Chronicles of the Shroud
Volume 1

The Messenger

Stefan Allen

&

Jerry Sword

Allen & Sword

Chronicles of the Shroud Volume 1 The Messenger

Copyright © 2013 Stefan Allen & Jerry Sword

Published by Full Moon Publishing, LLC

Glade Spring, VA

Webiste http://www.fullmoonpublishingllc.com/

ISBN: 0615895336
ISBN-13: 978-0615895338

Edited by Mary Klaus

Cover photos purchased from IStock Photo and designed by Jerry Sword

Allen & Sword

Dedication

To all through my life who have taught me, loved me, and lifted me up so that I could achieve this dream come true.

-S Allen

For the shining light of my life, of whom I become more proud every day, as I watch you chase your own dreams. I love you Jonathan.

-Jerry Sword

Allen & Sword

Chapter 1

The sun hung like a burning jewel, intent on setting the New Mexico horizon on fire with its ominous presence. The Plains of San Augustine lie between the towns of Magdalena and Datil. Out in the Plains, perched atop a radio telescope that was one of many in the Very Large Array, was a crow glaring unforgiving into the distance. Its eyes had witnessed the very essence of life and death in this rough environment. Out here, in his world, life and death was not a matter of sheer chance. It was quite simply survival of the fittest, or the sickest. As in most life forms, survival came down to how far one was willing to go to be the survivor. On this day *he* was the survivor. Now as he sat perched on top of one of the telescopes designed to find intelligent life "out there", many humans would be questioning whether or not there was actually intelligent life "down here". The crow however, being very intelligent, had fought his battles for the day, at least so far, and had won. He was now staring into the distance, as if he could see some seventy-five miles away into Albuquerque, where life went on for the human race, the people who seemed not to think in any critical manner for themselves, but to listen and accept whatever the biased leaders in their lives spouted out of their mouths. The crow knew that events were beginning to unfold that would affect not only Albuquerque, but the entire human population. Yes today he was the survivor. He was the fittest. He was the sickest.

The sound of high-heeled shoes clicking against a checkerboard tiled hallway floor subconsciously penetrated

Michael's dreams and caused him to stir. His body ached, as did his head. The repetitive clicking seemed to make this ache exponentially more miserable. The clicking drew dangerously close, and then stopped.

Michael lifted his head to find the thin figure of Lindsay Vivianni looking at him from the doorway of the cluttered cubicle. Lindsay was an attractive woman of Italian descent and although she was in her mid forties, her dark eyes and flawless complexion afforded her the ability to destroy hearts like a violent storm. Many men had found themselves emotionally scarred at her hands due to the fact that after divorcing a husband of nearly twenty years, Lindsay had decided to be a bit more selective in whom she would lay claims to this time out. Her inquisitive gaze made Michael a bit nervous. He looked at her and wondered why she was staring with such a questioning look in her eyes.

"Hello Lindsay, how are you this fine evening?" He decided small talk may be the best way to handle the situation at hand, yet found it impossible to disguise the sarcastic tone of his own voice.

"Mr. Reagan, we are not on a first name basis. For the last time you are to address me as Dr. Vivianni, as in Dr. Vivianni, Dean of the College of History. Are we clear?" she asked.

"Crystal" Michael ran his fingers through his disheveled hair and yawned.

"Do you have any idea what time it is?" She was being inquisitive again.

Mike stole a look at the hands on the clock hanging behind her.

"Almost eight o'clock; wow," Mike looked a bit embarrassed. "You're right Linds...I mean Doctor. I must have dozed off for a bit. I do apologize. Maybe I could make up for my oversight by buying you dinner? You can pick where we go." She appeared to be less than flattered by his sarcastic pick up line but the next words out of her mouth were definitely not what he expected to hear.

"Mr. Reagan" she paused for effect," It is almost eight o'clock *a.m.* You have been here all night."

This added an entirely new level of embarrassment and humiliation to Michael Reagan's current situation.

"Oh no...Not again." His face was now flushed.

"Mr. Reagan, I get very tired of reminding you that if you expect to have a position on this faculty in a few months then re-evaluating your priorities *is* in your best interest." She stared into his face never taking her eyes from his.

"You really don't have to remind me again Dr. Vivianni, I am very much aware of our current situation." He was on the verge of becoming defensive now.

"And your dissertation? How much longer until you complete it?"

Michael took a long look around him at all the books cluttering his space. In almost every nook and corner of his small cubicle there was a somewhat unorganized heaping pile of books. Some were paper backed, some were bound by leather, and some were so old that the print could not be easily deciphered. Aside from the normal reference materials that any writer should keep close at hand, the bulk of them ranged in topics concerning medieval history. There were books about rulers. There were books about regions. There were books about crusades and empires. Behind the vast expanses of this ten by twelve foot library the body of Michael Reagan had been lying, face down and dozing for most of the early morning hours. Now he had been forced to awaken not only to the grand inquisition from the lovely Dr. Vivianni but also to the one repetitive question that had influenced his decision to give up and pass out in the first place. *What am I doing here?*

Michael had been struggling to complete his PhD dissertation for some time now; however he had not always led such a mediocre existence. For the past three years he had studied to be the best in his field and could not help the simple fact that somewhere along the way he had basically lost the initiative that burned inside him at the beginning, which he now considered to be the beginning of the end. The fact was that he had spent the last several months reading things he never even cared about in the first place, struggling to get caught up in the process that he had ignored when he began his research. Now as he looked up at Dr. Vivianni's inquisitive, beautiful gaze, thoughts of his former life came flooding into his mind. The dam had been breached.

He remembered what it had been like to teach high school. He remembered what it was like to meet new

4

people, to interact with his students and fellow teachers, and to have a life. He remembered summers spent abroad and what it was like to get drunk and wake up with strange and exotic women. He had explored Europe during one of those summers, spending time in every city, as well as finding female companionship in most of them, at least for one night. It was only upon moving to Belgrade, Serbia that he finally fell in love with the people, the places, and the history. His love for this place became so strong in fact that he returned every summer for the next three years, always wanting to know more, and always exploring. He found great intrigue in the stories of the men and women who struggled through time in this place.

Then he met Juliana. Oh god! Juliana! She could have been the very breath of god himself. He had lived with her during the last summer he had been there. During this summer she began telling him about how the Renaissance had begun in Serbia, instead of in Italy like the textbooks had taught. At first he had doubted her until she showed him the undeniable proof. Between exploring new restaurants and coffee shops they explored each other: in bed, in city parks, and even once in an elevator. The more museums they searched the fonder of this Serbian Renaissance idea Michael had become. In fact the fascination engulfed him. The passion had been ignited and burned as bright as the New Mexico sun that was now making a steady ascent into the morning sky. Life had been good. So good, in fact, that as with every great empire in history, it eventually imploded upon itself. Since he had enjoyed teaching so much it only made sense to him to pursue an advanced degree and teach on a university level. More money, more prestige, more life! Right?

WRONG! Life had become a total nightmare on too many levels. There were too many hoops to jump through, there was too much red tape and there were too many politics involved in this quest. There were too many professors, both women and men, who would have easily given this student any grade he wanted in return for sexual gratification. It all left him with the very real feeling that the only thing he needed to do to insure a future position on the faculty was to kiss the right ass, both figuratively and literally. With his passion still burning inside of him, Michael had returned to the university to explore his new ideas, and he was still sitting there today, with no dissertation. The desire to research was now only a glowing ember of a distant memory that felt used and sterile, not so different than the memories of him and Juliana trying to make love and instead just grunting and grinding each other five times a night in five different places. The glamour was gone.

There was only one possible solution to reigniting the fire that had once been irrepressible, Michael Reagan had to get back to Belgrade. He could research there and try to find Juliana once again. It seemed like a maddening daydream, but then it quickly evolved into something else. He turned it over and over in his mind until it actually seemed like a great idea. He could spend the summer there and return in the fall to lock himself away once more, and write for the entire final semester. This idea excited him

and this very idea snapped him back to the moment at hand, and the glare from Dr. Vivianni.

"Mr. Reagan! I'm only going to ask you one more time! What is it going to take to make you take this seriously?"

Michael looked dumbfounded, and then found his resolve.

"Leaving." His voice was barely audible to her. He seemed to be speaking more to himself than to her. He turned to face her once more, seeing the questioning look in her eyes.

"Lindsay, I need to get out of here" he said as he stood and began hurriedly gathering his things.

"You're right," she said, "Go get some rest before you come back here." She was talking as he walked away from her down the long corridor. He was now in a hurry and she could not figure out the reason.

"I'll see you tomorrow Mr. Reagan?" she was quizzing him again. He stopped walking and turned to face her.

"I'll see you in the fall instead," he said.

"What? Are you losing your mind?" she was visibly confused.

"No, not yet anyway," he assured her although she did not necessarily believe his words to be the truth.

"Where are you going?" The morning light shone in her eyes and she was beautiful.

For a moment she saw a determination on his face she had not seen before. It caught her off guard, and to her embarrassment, made her feel aroused.

"Belgrade," he said, "I have to get back to Belgrade." Michael Reagan turned and walked down the hall and out the double doors into the New Mexico heat.

Lindsay Vivianni's jaw hit the university floor, although only for a brief moment. She regained herself quickly as she stood and watched him go. She was speechless and breathless at the same time.

Michael got to his car. While he was fumbling for his keys and had his hands full of the detritus he had taken from his office, the full enormity of all of this morning and of his life hit him like bricks falling out of the sky. He barely got the car door open, the stuff thrown in the backseat before he slumped into the driver's seat and just started crying.

He just couldn't do this anymore. He could not go back into that cubicle and read another article on some historian's examination of a pimple on the ass of some other historian. He couldn't face Lindsay again with nothing and less than nothing with each passing day. He couldn't face the emptiness of his life. He couldn't face life.

Michael cried, he wept loudly and deeply. Darkness entered his car and his heart and he could see no way to get out. He was a very long way from Belgrade.

Eventually Michael dried his wet cheeks and started the car. The radio came on and a song, his song, no, their song came on. The song that he and Julianna had danced to, all that summer, was blaring throughout the car. Light came on in his heart, he knew again what he must do. Belgrade was a requirement, not an option, and not a daydream.

Michael backed out of the parking lot and drove, singing the song as loudly as he could all the way home.

He opened the door of his apartment, a dilapidated place where many grad students had lived throughout the years and where the wreckage of many lives had found walls to live in. He saw immediately what he had needed to see: the photo of Julianna and himself, taken that special summer, next to the Danube River. They were on the balcony of that coffee shop they enjoyed so much.

As Michael walked into the house his mind went back to that summer:

The day had been cloudy but warm. He and Julianna had walked the cobblestone streets of the old city looking at the architecture and enjoying the company of each other. One or the other would pull towards the open door of a shop and they would both go in. They would look around, laugh at various items and then walk out, to continue down the cobblestone street. In one place she had pulled him into a tobacco shop and they had chosen one cigar to share. The man behind the counter snipped it and lit it for them. They walked out of the shop sharing the cigar, puffing, blowing smoke and laughing as they held each other tight with arms around each others' waist.

They walked further to the central square. Here there was a street magician and also a jazz band. The tuba player held his tuba together with grey duct tape. But he played well as a little boy of about 13 years old sang blues and jazz. The two lovers stood with smiles and pure, simple enjoyment. As it began to sprinkle with rain, they headed around the corner to a coffee shop.

As they sat on the balcony, with a coffee each and some powered pastries, Michael had looked into Juliana's eyes and known that he loved her. Those green eyes and the handmade earrings he had just bought her that afternoon captured the withering sunlight. An Asian woman set up to play the violin on the outside edge of the shop. As she played, they drank coffee and looked out over the Danube River. This was the greatest moment Michael had ever had in his life.

An older German couple had walked by and Michael asked if they would snap a picture. They did.

This was the photograph Michael had on his wall in his dingy place. This was the photo that Michael was still staring at as the sun moved to the West and shadows crept in the corners. This was the photograph Michael was still staring at when the firm and complete resolution was made

in his heart to make a drastic move. *A requirement, NOT an option.*

      Michael walked into the bathroom and washed his hands. He looked in the mirror and for the first time in several weeks actually looked at the man reflected back through its surface. A man mid-thirties, unruly brown (was it still brown even with a few strands of white or grey?) hair. He needed a haircut. He had tried a beard some weeks ago, but right now no hair covered his face. Some wrinkles were beginning around his eyes, but still those blue eyes with their crystal centers moved the ladies. For his age, and compared to other men in early midlife, he looked pretty good. Still fit, a small paunch, but his 6 foot 2 inch frame could hold its own still in a game of basketball against his 18 year old nephew.

      Michael set up his laptop, got online and purchased an airline ticket for Belgrade. He then emailed Julianna that he would arrive at her apartment at 11am in three days. He then emailed Lindsay and told her he would see her in late August. He emailed his parents and brother that he would be doing research in Serbia and that he might not be in touch for a while. As Michael closed his email account, a sudden and deep tiredness came over him. He slumped down on the couch and went to a deep sleep. Figments of dreams, of changes, of excitement filtered into his tired mind as his body never moved through the night. *NOT an option.*

Chapter 2

Michael sat in the center of the aisle as the plane took off. The deserts of New Mexico fell from underneath the aircraft as they began to blend into the sandy landscape. The blue sky was all he could see through the windows as the earth fell out from under him and the craft. The United Airlines flight from Albuquerque to Belgrade would consist of just over thirty-seven hours of travel, making stops in Los Angeles, Philadelphia, and Frankfurt, Germany. Although flying was not his favorite mode of travel, Michael sighed with obvious relief as he leaned back in his seat and somehow managed to nod off to sleep. His elbows bumped against the fat man in the seat next to him. He was now dreaming as if he were lecturing in a class.

"We have all been taught from grade school that the Renaissance, the "Enlightenment", began in Italy. Such greats as Leonardo da Vinci, Michelangelo and all those others somehow woke up one morning and felt rather enlightened." There were a few snickers and giggles from some of the students as Michael emphasized the word enlightened. He paused for a moment before continuing. "They threw off the yoke of the "dark ages" and felt renewed. They began writing in a manner to show the humanity of men and women. They began painting and sculpting to show the beauty of the human form. These men began to develop ideas, thoughts and philosophies to declare that humans were the epitome of all in the universe.

Well that whole idea class, is not how it happened."

The class was now taken aback as if their professor was speaking blasphemous words and that he was defying everything they had been taught.

"It seems that the Empire of Serbia was a pocket of Europe where men learned and grew in knowledge. These men were on the cusp of the Ottoman Empire, what with the entire Middle East only across a river or two, and had at their disposal the knowledge of the Persians, Greeks, Romans and 1000 years of Ottoman and Arab thought and research. Recall, these Arabs discovered the zero, modern mathematics, astronomy and historical methods of scientific research. These monks in Serbia translated and studied. They read of the teachings of Confucius from China. They read of the teachings of the Buddha. Their minds were stretched from the isolated teachings of their church. These teachings expanded into new ideas expressed in writings, art, sculpture, paintings and a beginning of a belief that humans are indeed special and full of light and truth. The seeds of what we have come to know as the Italian Renaissance were beginning to sprout."

Some of the students that initially thought Professor Reagan had lost his mind were now captivated with his lecture, feeding off every word.

"But, alas history intrudes. A massive Ottoman army invades Serbia about this time and destroys the Empire, the King and the monasteries. Some of the monks escaped across the sea to Italy. Does everyone in here understand? The seeds go to Italy and the rest is history!

The remainders are killed, research destroyed and blackness descends for 500 years upon Serbia...

Now, class, this is the truth of history. Hinges of history happen. Enlightenment began in Serbia but armies pushed it, shoved it, and forced it to Italy. In Italy it flourished, grew and spread to the entire world." He spoke with authority and vast understanding, quite the accomplished professor...

Something, someone, hit Michael's elbow and he awoke. Several hours and a change of planes in Germany had passed, along with a couple of movies. Raising the window shade he found sunlight and land outside. Standing in the long line in the narrow aisle to exit the plane, Michael felt relief as he breathed again the fragrant (at least in his own mind) air of Serbia. He was home. This was where life changed. He was determined to make things, all things, different this time in Serbia.

Outside the aerodrome Michael rented a car, and began the drive to Juliana's last known address. She had not answered any emails he had sent from his home while he was packing, from the various airports, nor from the plane via his iPad. He hoped beyond all hope that she might still be around. He parked up the block from her apartment. Michael grabbed his bag and began walking down the familiar street. He looked around and was reminded of places they had spent time, as vivid memories washed over him. There was the alley where they shared their first kiss, the coffee shop where he would often go in the mornings, while she was at work, to drink, talk, write and enjoy the

entire ambience of the locale, and the neighbors: the old man with the brown hat, the young lady who was pregnant, the twins who always asked for candy. Arriving at her door, he was told by the lady inside that no one lives there by that name. Michael looked around again, his vision now set in the present, instead of the eyes of several summers ago. He looked around, seeing the neighborhood, and realized a lot had changed. Two wars, attacks by NATO and embargoes had forced movement of people and ideas yet again.

The people walking in the streets seemed a bit more ragged than he remembered. Several of the stores and cafes up and down the street were closed and boarded up. Even the street seemed dirtier and the buildings needed maintenance. Too many years had passed in this street and in his heart.

He turned again to the woman at the door while she continued to look at him. He was now smiling.

"I knew Julianna who lived in this apartment several years ago." He explained, "She and I spent a summer together. I was hoping she was still here."

Also with a smile, the young woman began telling him just a bit of her own story, "I just moved here only a year ago. I do not know what happened before that. In fact, this entire neighborhood was almost empty when I arrived. All of these people have been here only a short time. I am so sorry your friend is not here."

Looking Michael over and seeing his dejected manner, she interjected, "Would you like to come in for a coffee?"

Michael walked inside; his shoulders slumped, with complete lack of hope. He felt as if he might end up seeing Lindsay, *Dr. Vivianni*, sooner than he had really wanted or anticipated.

He walked through the familiar door already knowing where the living room was and continued to look around. All had changed, but there was still a familiarity to the room and to the place that was almost eerie. He was walking with ghosts.

"I am Sladjana. I am from a small village a few hours north of here. But I came here for my job. I am an internet technologist. After some years working in Canada, I came here last year to begin my life in the "big" city." She paused to follow Michael's gaze, and then continued, "I see you looking at my musical instruments. Yes, I play the violin and guitar. I play the violin in the local orchestra and the guitar for friends." She laughed and he discovered very quickly that he liked the way she smiled.

Michael and Sladjana shared coffee and exchanged travel stories. He told her how he had traveled and researched across Europe but had fallen in love with the people and history of Serbia. She told him of her studies at the university, how growing up in a small village had birthed a deep desire to live in the vastness of a city, and of her travels working with the   Blackberry Corporation in

Toronto for a year and how this experience of living in Canada and visiting America had changed her life. Although invited to remain in Canada to work and build a life, she purposely chose to return to her Serbia and help build her nation in her small way.

Sladjana loved how this man showed such an intense interest in the history of her country. She also liked the way he looked at her with those piercing blue eyes. Michael looked at her and simply enjoyed the very act of conversation with this woman; she was an intense and active participant in life and this thrilled him.

Michael couldn't help but become dumbfounded in this house. He came all this way to try to find Julianna, but instead he had discovered this astonishing woman; at least she looked this way on the outside, and Michael really wanted her to be a wonderful woman on the inside too. She was a woman with shoulder length brown hair, stunning brown eyes, and a smile to bring sunshine into any situation, more of a sideways grin of pleasure and whimsicalness all combined.

They continued to drink coffee and after about an hour of stories, Michael knew it was time to leave and make an attempt to find his way.

As Sladjana closed the door, she peeked out the window to watch Michael walk down the street. She smiled to herself, and had he been able to see her, he would have noticed a twinkle of mischief in her eye.

Michael found a hotel and began moving in. He also started to plan his moves of research, and decided to get a feel for the history of the city. He eventually left the hotel and walked along the old city wall. His path took him along the center square where kings and princes reigned through the centuries. He planned to hire a car and drive to the Kosovo Polje (Kosovo Plain - "field of the black birds") where in 1389, the vassal troops, with Bosnian, Montenegrin, Bulgarian and other allies, commanded by Prince Lazar Hrebeljanovic - the strongest regional ruler in Serbia at the time - suffered defeat. This was the place where that fateful king gave away his army to the invading Turkish army, and thus destroyed his own kingdom.

But first he made a phone call to the number that once was Juliana's, hoping that Sladjana would pick up. Much to his surprise she answered his call. His heart skipped a beat.

"Would you possibly know of any nice place for dinner tonight? I'm still getting my bearings and I can't recall most of the restaurants right now? And, also, I hate to eat alone, would you like to go with me to dinner?" he asked as if she had already rejected him.

Sladjana, however, was pleasantly surprised "Yes, there is a small pizza shop just around the corner from the main square. You do remember where the main square is, don't you?"

"Of course" she heard through the phone.

"Good. It is simple, but the pizzas are the best in the city. And, yes, I will go with you *just* so you do not have to eat alone." She laughed with girlish innocence, and he liked what he heard.

Michael agreed to meet her in two hours then returned to his hotel to freshen up. He was still making plans for his research. This would only be a minor and well deserved delay, however brief a delay it was.

Sladjana disconnected the phone from Michael and stood there thinking. She really did not know this guy. He just dropped into her life with a story. Her mother had taught her better than this. She needed to see who this Michael guy really was.

Fadia, a reporter for Aljazeera News out of Qatar, had been her friend since they were in grade school together. Fadia would certainly have resources to quickly check up on this guy and tell Sladjana if she should continue to see him in any capacity.

Fadia and Sladjana talked for several minutes while Fadia searched the database for Michael Reagan. She found the same information he had given with no surprises. Sladjana was now much more at peace in meeting him for dinner.

Fadia made a note to check further on what this guy Michael and her friend Sladjana might be doing. She was a good reporter because she never let any small piece of information slide away.

Sladjana was simply stunning in black pants, a white sleeveless top and purple lacy shawl across her shoulders. They drove to the main square, parked and ambled down the length of the square. They talked; they laughed, and they got to know each other, both seeming to be having a genuinely good time.

As Michael thought about the conversation that night, he realized they both had moved quickly in their conversation from safe, easy topics like family, where they lived, music and movies, to more personal topics such as life dreams, mistakes they made in the work place, in love lives, in personal lives. Some of this was funny and they both laughed. Some was sad and tears came. But on a very deep level these two had touched and enjoyed touching the spirit and soul of each other.

They finished eating; then finished a bottle of wine while sitting under the stars, holding each other close against the coolness of the summer evening that came with a breeze from across the Danube River.

He took her home and she asked him to come in for a coffee. Against his better judgment, he declined telling her he had to rise early the next morning to begin his research. He promised there would be another time for late evening coffee. They kissed a simple kiss and he made his way back to the hotel.

The next day Michael was driving towards the valley. These roads were steep and full of curves. Few of them were paved. Michael took his time and drove slowly as he looked back and forth across the landscape that had been full of armies and travelling people for thousands of years. He had already driven by the huge Studenica Monastery, built about 1190. A few miles down the road, he looked across a cattle field and noticed a stone wall with part of a tower behind it. Since he enjoyed walking around and also touching old works, he drove to the side of the road and walked through the field to this ancient building.

As he drew closer, he realized that it looked like a church or a monastery. This particular monastery was not on his map and looked quite old, dilapidated and in disrepair. He pulled out his iPad and began research on the possibilities of this place. He discovered it was Saint Prohar of Christ Monastery; built about 1150 to honor Saint Prochorus after his prophesy failed. But the saint lived an exemplary life and spent it; since his prophesy to gain the Serbian throne failed and his political career thus ended, helping others and gathering a library for others to use to gain knowledge. These buildings were not the impressive monastery built for this saint by the Byzantine emperor Romanus IV. This was a gathering of a few small buildings hidden behind a hill in a small valley. It was insignificant and not noteworthy. One could understand how it had been neglected and ignored for seemingly centuries. It had been built just 50 odd years before the men of the Fourth Crusade (1202- 1204) rode and walked through this valley towards Constantinople.

Michael began to look around the grounds and walls of the monastery. Almost all the buildings were more in disrepair than repair. The walls around the place were broken down and grass grew everywhere. It looked as if no one had bothered about this religious place in hundreds of years. He noticed the graffiti of previous visitors. These were soldiers, knights, and peasants who traveled from Central and Western Europe on their way to the Fourth Crusade to invade Constantinople. These men and some women had travelled from all of Europe towards Egypt. But when the ships expected in Venice would not take them to Egypt (the backdoor to attack the Arabians in the Holy Land), the army decided to attack Constantinople and take the riches of this last Roman city to their homes in Europe.

Men had written on the stones:

"God bless us as we walk with Him"

"Prince Phillip was here and prayed"

"Where is God? I miss my home"

Scratched into the stones were prayers, curses, sayings of men and some women who passed through these walls going from their homes throughout Europe and then returning from the horrors of war with darkness engraved in their hearts.

Michael came to the realization that this monastery was a stop -over for the crusaders as they drew near to the huge eastern Roman Empire city in modern day Turkey. These men were going to their deaths. It was 1202. They had sacked the city of Constantinople, and taken the riches when factions of the army turned on one another and began killing each other to gain more riches for themselves. The Roman Empire was finalized with the destruction of Constantinople.

So these men, those who survived must have passed through here on their way back home. But the European army had fractured and those who had gathered at this monastery might have been hiding from other parts of the army coming up to kill them and take their riches. The invading army was close on their heels, but they likely left messages as they were hiding from the other Crusaders.

Michael began to look around. He was reading graffiti, looking through rooms and pausing often to just get the feel of the place in those days of history. Men were scared and grieving over losing friends, princes, faith in God and feared that the army behind them would follow them to their homes and thus kill their own families looking to gather more of the riches of the old Roman Empire city. Surely some of these men had taken riches and treasures from the destroyed city. Constantinople had been the seat of the Roman Empire for a thousand years. Gold, silver, precious stones, art and artifacts were stored in that city. Surely some of this, plus the writings from the grand library, had come through this place.

Michael moved cautiously to the interior of the buildings and towards the altar area. Crawling over stones that had fallen from walls, holding on to small trees that had grown through the stone floor, and finally arriving at the altar, he grew silent and pensive in his soul. He knelt down to pray; just as so many of those men had done 800 years before. Loss, anxiety, grief, hopelessness, fear and failure washed over them and now him. He bowed his head on the stone steps with tears welling in his eyes. The soldiers had begun their journey full of hope, joy and a bright future. They returned to this monastery, this altar, in fear that their lives were now closed and at an end. Michael felt their pain and he felt a release of the pain, fears and hopelessness of his own empty, meaningless life. He bowed, wept and then lay prostrate on the grooved stone floor at the edge of the altar. Heaven help him.

Minutes passed and he finally opened his eyes to find that right there, faintly, on the steps was an arrow, smooth with time, but definitely an arrow, pointing towards the altar. Michael thought he wasn't seeing clearly through his own tears. He dried his eyes and looked again. Yes. There was definitely an arrow. He looked around to see if anyone else had walked in. There was no one. He was completely alone on this single still frame of time, feeling the pain of centuries and lives gone by, and feeling the pain of the here and now. He crawled on his knees with his nose inches away from the stone step and followed the arrow, looking for something else. At the edge of the stone altar was a smaller scratch. It looked remarkably like the other arrow, but much smaller; still pointing underneath the altar.

He placed his hands on the altar and pushed. Without much effort, he moved the stone structure a few feet. A stone on the floor under the altar was loose. He applied force and the stone easily came out of the floor. Peering into its dark resting place he discovered that under the stone was a leather bag. Again he looked around. He could hear his own heart beating out of his chest.

Michael put his hands into the bag and felt what he already knew to be a parchment. He removed it carefully, oh so very carefully. He took extra caution so as not to harm the precious document in any way. He looked at the parchment and tears again welled up in his eyes. He knew this document had not been seen by the human eye for quite some time to say the least. Many generations had passed right by it and many lifetimes had passed since it had even seen the light of day.

Chapter 3

I, Branislav, a humble monk, in the year of our Lord 1205, sit to write this letter. It is a dark time and I pray that God, in all His glory, might come and bring grace and mercy to this wretched place.

I have been in this order for 45 years. I came as a young man, with my heart toward God and a desire to serve Him only. I have learned to read and write, and have even translated many texts from all over the world. Now, as this day dawns, I am the abbot of this order, in this small valley, behind these hills, by the grace of God.

The Crusading army has returned in disarray and fear from the armies that destroyed Constantinople. This fear came as the leaders of the Christian armies began to attack and destroy the other European armies in order to steal more treasures for their own lords and ladies back home. They tell me the city has fallen. The great churches and texts have been desecrated. Priests and believers have been tortured and murdered.

Prince Phillip has returned mortally wounded. His wound is green and I fear he will live only a few more days. He has given me a divine treasure and asked me to hide it and lock away its secrets forever. I have been forbidden to look within the leather bag; and instructed to seal it in the crypt and then leave this holy place before the other knights and armies arrive.

I am sorry for the delay. Several days have passed since the above was written. The Prince is dead. His knights have buried him. I spoke several masses for his immortal soul.

As for the leather bag, after his death, alone in my chambers, I prayed and then feeling compelled by Almighty God Himself, I opened the bag. Inside was a light. It was dark in my rooms, but the inside had a glow.

I put my hand within the bag and felt linen, of fine quality. I removed this linen from the bag and the linen itself was glowing, brighter than a candle. My chambers were aglow with supernatural light.

I unfolded the linen and found what I can only describe as the burial shroud of our Lord and Savior Jesus Christ.

His face, dear God! Your face, so beautiful, so kingly, so majestic, had left impressions from the dirt and blood that covered it before you left this world. The blood stains from the wounds on your head, your hands, your side and then your feet were all clearly left behind even when you had risen from the tomb.

I am the first man in 1200 years to gaze upon your face, my Lord. I fear I will die.

I was overcome with awe and worship. I could not write. I had to meditate and   pray.

27

But now I have returned and with a plan. We all know the armies will soon be approaching. Our scouts warn of only two or three more days before they arrive to destroy all they can see.

I cannot allow this treasure, this gift, this holy relic to go into the hands of these knights who seek only treasure and not the ways of God. I must do all within my power to protect it.

I am an old man and I cannot travel fast. I have been inside this monastery for too many years and no longer know the ways of the world. There is no one around me I can trust with so great a treasure.

If I run with this gift, I will be caught and killed. And the treasure will fall into their hands.

If you are reading this letter then know that I am dead. I will leave this place with a false shroud (some soldiers created such a linen shroud from some old linen they found in the great city).

I leave the authentic shroud of the Lord in this place. I place it in a place only a holy man will discover. I cannot say more, for if the heathen or these renegade knights find this letter, then all is lost.

I pray for you my brother. You are entrusted with the greatest gift the world has ever known. You have the gift of life. Walk carefully, for the hour is dark.

Chapter 4

Michael sat in the darkness trying desperately to recall the texts he had been so reluctant to stay awake for. Now the memories were washing over him in waves. His head was reeling, yet somehow through the flashes inside his mind's eye, he recalled information from articles that were now laying half a world away. He opened these articles on his iPad and began perusing what he already knew but needed to confirm.

"Researcher claims Shroud of Turin is genuine"

By STEPHANIE DAVIS, APP

ROME – Researchers within the Vatican claim a nearly transparent text on the Shroud of Turin proves the authenticity of the ancient artifact revered as the burial cloth of Jesus. The claim made in a new book by historian Dianna Greer has drawn skepticism from some scientists, who maintain the shroud is a medieval forgery. Greer leads a research team at the Vatican archives, and during a press conference said that she used computers to enhance images of faintly written words scattered across the shroud. The words were written in Greek, Latin, and Aramaic.

According to Greer, the words include the name "Jesus Nazarene" written in Greek, proving the text could not be of medieval origin because no Christian at the time, even a forger, would have labeled Jesus a Nazarene without referring to his divinity. The shroud bears the image of a crucified man, complete with blood seeping out of nailed hands and feet. Believers say Christ's image was recorded on the linen fibers at the time of the resurrection. The fragile artifact is kept locked in a special protective chamber in Turin's cathedral and is rarely shown by the Vatican. Skeptics still affirm that radiocarbon dating conducted in 1988 determined the cloth was made in the 13th or 14th century.

Faint letters scattered around the face on the burial cloth were discovered decades ago, however serious researchers dismissed them due to the results of the radiocarbon dating. Greer states that when she cut out the words from photos of the shroud and showed them to experts, they all agreed that the writing style was typical of the Middle East in the first century. She believes the text was written on a document and glued to the shroud so that the body could be identified by relatives and receive a proper burial. She also believes that metals in the ink being used at the time may have allowed the writing to transfer to the linen.

Greer claims the text also partially confirms the Gospels' account of Jesus' final moments. She states that a fragment in Greek which translates to the phrase "removed at the ninth hour" may refer to Christ's time of death reported in the biblical texts. Greer has studied enhanced images of the shroud, where at least seven words can be seen, fragmented and scattered on and around the image of the face, crisscrossing the cloth vertically and horizontally. There is one short sequence of Aramaic letters that has not been translated, while another Latin fragment — "iber" — may refer to Emperor Tiberius, who reigned at the time of Jesus' crucifixion.

Dr. Greer asserts that she remains objective in her findings with all religious aspects set aside, noting that what she is certain of is that the shroud is the documentation of the execution of a man in a specific time and place. Greer has gained recognition in Italy for her research on the medieval order of the Knights Templar and her discovery of unpublished documents pertaining to the group within the Vatican's archives.

…Another flash in his mind carried him back to yet another article…

"ROME (Presswire) – An Italian scientist claims to have reproduced the Shroud of Turin, a feat that he says proves the linen some Christians revere as Jesus Christ's burial cloth, is a medieval forgery. The shroud, which measures a little over 14 feet by 3 feet, bears the image of a crucified man some believers say is Christ.

"We have shown that it is possible to reproduce a cloth which has the same characteristics as the Shroud of Turin," Mario Garlas, who will be discussing the results at a conference this weekend in northern Italy, said on Monday. A professor of organic chemistry at the University of Pavia, Garlas made available to various news organizations the paper he will deliver as well as the accompanying comparative photographs.

The Shroud of Turin shows the image of a bearded man with long hair, his arms crossed over his chest, while the entire

31

linen cloth is marked by what appears to be rivulets of blood from wounds in the wrists, feet, and side. These wounds appear to be similar to the wounds Christ suffered during the crucifixion. Carbon dating tests conducted by laboratories in 1988 caused a sensation by dating the cloth from between 1260 and 1390. Skeptics claimed it was a hoax, and was possibly made to attract the profitable medieval pilgrimage business. Scientists, however, have yet to explain how the image was left on the cloth.

Garlas reproduced the full-sized shroud using materials and techniques that would have been available during the Middle Ages. He placed a linen sheet over a volunteer and then rubbed it with a pigment containing small amounts of acid. The pigment was then artificially aged by heating the cloth in an oven and washing it. This process removed the stain from the surface, leaving a half-tone image similar to the one on the Shroud of Turin. He then added blood stains, burn holes, scorches and water stains to achieve the final desired effect.

The Shroud of Turin is one of the most disputed and controversial relics in Christianianity. It is locked away at Turin Cathedral in Italy and rarely exhibited.

After surfacing in the Middle East and France, it was brought by Italy's former royal family, the Savoys, to their seat in Turin in 1578. In 1983 ex-King Umberto II bequeathed it to the late Pope John Paul. The burial cloth escaped destruction in 1997 when a fire ravaged the Guarini Chapel of the Turin Cathedral where it is held. It was saved by a fireman who   risked his life. "

Michael had read these news articles and many more like them. He had sat down by the altar with the leather bag close at his side; he needed to spend a lot more time online looking for anything that might help him in his quest to discover just what he had found. He had read how the history of the Shroud of Turin was lost through time, how it surfaced in odd times, and how the provenance was never authenticated. He was lost in thought, contemplation and even prayer as the day had grown dark.

Michael wanted to know more. He clutched the leather bag tightly and held to it as if his life depended on it while he made his way back to his hotel. He powered up his laptop and went to Wikipedia to get an overview of the Shroud. A few keystrokes later, and after the dreadful warning "You've got mail," Michael's monitor came alive with more information.

The Image of Edessa

This image, which dates back to the 10th century, shows Abgarus of Edessa displaying the Image of Edessa. The oblong cloth shown here is unusual for depictions of the image, leading some to speculate that the artist was influenced by seeing the Shroud of Turin.

The Gospel of John states that the Apostle Peter and the "beloved disciple" entered the tomb of Jesus shortly after his resurrection, of which they were still unaware, and found the "linen clothes" that had wrapped his body along

33

with "the napkin, that was about his head."

There are multiple reports of the shroud Christ was wrapped in, or an image of his head, being venerated in various locations prior to the fourteenth century. However, none of these reports has been connected with any certainty to the Shroud of Turin.

There are three key pieces of evidence which are cited in favor of identification with the Shroud of Turin. In his work On Holy Images, Saint John of Damascus refers to the Edessa image as being a strip of oblong cloth, rather than a square, as other accounts of the Edessa cloth. He does, however, still speak of the image of Jesus' face when he was alive.

To the contrary, a panel of experts on Late Antique and Byzantine History at the University of Oxford deny the possibility of the Turin shroud being identified with the Image of Edessa. Among other reasons, http://en.wikipedia.org/wiki/Shroud_of_Turin - cite_note-21 *The Image of Edessa, according to them, has its origin in the resistance to the Byzantine iconoclasm.*http://en.wikipedia.org/wiki/Shroud_of_Turin - cite_note-22

A specific image from a Hungarian manuscript dates from 1192 to 1195. Shroud advocates cite this as evidence for the shroud's existence before the fourteenth century, proclaiming that an L-shaped patch near the hands also corresponds to four burn holes in the relic. The weave of the cloth in the lower panel also suggests to them the unusual weave of the shroud.

When the cloth was transferred to Constantinople in 944, Gregory Referendarius, the archdeacon of Hagia Sophia in Constantinople, preached a sermon about the artifact. "

"So," Michael stopped and pondered on this, "the Shroud seems to have been in Constantinople before the Fourth Crusade!" Then he continued reading.

"The sermon itself had been lost but was rediscovered in the Vatican Archives and translated by Richard Drake in 2003. The document states that the Edessa cloth contained not only the face, but also a full-length image of the body. Other documents have since been found in the Vatican library and the University of Leiden, Netherlands, which confirm this impression.

In 1203, a Crusader knight made claims the cloth was among the countless relics in Constantinople, and that every Friday the cloth would raise itself into an upright position making the full image visible to anyone who may be within sight of it.

"What?" He was thinking again, "A Fourth Crusader knight writes about seeing the cloth when Constantinople fell? Could the note from Brother Branislav have some truth? This was the same year Branislav wrote the letter! Oh God!"

In a letter sent to Pope Innocent III by Theodore

Angelos, a nephew of one of three Byzantine Emperors who were deposed during the Fourth Crusade, Angelos objects the attack on the capital. The document, dated 1 August 1205 reads: "The Venetians partitioned the treasures of gold, silver, and ivory while the French did the same with the relics of the saints and the most sacred of all, the linen in which our Lord Jesus Christ was wrapped after his death and before the resurrection. We know that the sacred objects are preserved by their predators in Venice, in France, and in other places, the sacred linen in Athens."

Michael was now talking to himself. "So someone thought they had gotten a hold of the Shroud and took it to Venice. They took the fake shroud Branislav wrote about." He stood and ran his fingers through his dark hair in frustration. "What if the real shroud were still hidden in the monastery? How is this possible?" He continued reading.

The location of the Image of Edessa since the 13th century is unknown, unless it is the Shroud of Turin.

Some historians suggest that the shroud was captured by the knight Otto de la Roche, but that he soon relinquished it to the Knights Templar. It was then taken to France, where the first known keeper of the Turin Shroud had connections to the Templars as well as the descendants of Otto. There is speculation that the shroud could have been a major part of the legendary "Templar Treasure" that treasure hunters still search for in modern times.

The association with the Templars seems to be based on a coincidence of family names; the Templars were a celibate order and very unlikely to have children after entering the Order. However, the location of the Shroud in the 13th and 14th centuries is interesting because the French contingent in the 4th Crusade, which resulted in the sack of Constantinople, was led by Tibaut of Champagne. Lirey, the first known location of the Turin Shroud, is located in the territory of this Count....

Michael knew he had come across something special in too many ways. Even basic research showed some kind of hope that perhaps something divine had happened here all those years ago. What had truly happened to cause the letter to be written, to cause the Abbot to run for his life, to cause this monastery to be destroyed and forgotten; would take much further research and sifting through the dust of history. Was he correct in what he was thinking or was he just going overboard with an imagination that he could not control?

It was dark; Michael grew very frightened; if this garment held the history that he thought it might, men would kill for it. And many would die for it as well. It was impossible to know how many already had. Perhaps this was how Branislav had met his end. Branislav and Michael Reagan were now connected through the sands of time. Michael made a promise to himself that he would accomplish one thing, he would stay alive. He was a long way from New Mexico indeed.

Chapter 5

Michael held the letter in his trembling hand. My God! From tears, smiles, fear and astonishment, Michael moved through those feelings in a spiraling circle. He looked around his hotel room, and for the first time he feared the oppressive darkness gathering around him. The day was far spent in a desolate place. Before returning to the hotel, while walking to the car, he turned around, gripping the leather bag in his hand, and gazed upon the buildings behind the hill. He had thought about Brother Branislav and how he must have gazed in the same way as he walked away from everything he had known for most of his life, walking into his certain death. How far did he get before events and evil men chased him down? A shiver went up Michael's spine, and part of it still remained.

Michael had driven carefully, not wanting to disturb the letter, his thoughts or the tumble of avalanching feelings going through his mind. He arrived at the hotel and locked the door, shoving a chair under the door knob before sitting on the bed. He trembled from so many emotions smashing their way through his body, mind and being. He consciously tried to stop the trembling, trying to get his mind under control and then he tried to relax, even a little bit.

He began fingering the leather bag while just sitting and thinking. Too many questions were going through his mind. He was thinking as a researcher, trained in philosophical thought and critical thinking. He was thinking as a rational man with all the feelings and fears coursing through him. He was thinking as one possessed with a grand, but fearful gift. Questions threw themselves against the inside of his brain:

What has happened to me?

What is this bag, this letter, this story?

Why me?

Oh, my god, what am I going to do?

Does anyone know?

Whom can I tell about this?

What do I do now?

These questions and many more, but all in this same vein, spiraled around him. He looked in the shadows of the room for any signs. He listened for sounds of hope, fear, someone outside the room. He was still a ball of tension as he laid his head upon the pillow and lied very still, trying to listen, relax and sleep.

Tiredness finally overwhelmed Michael. He dozed fitfully as the hours of the night passed. The letter and the leather bag lay on the bed next to him. Finally, he slept.

Slowly as Michael sank into deep slumber, his mind broke free from his body and a dream seemed to come into his mind, his spirit, and his very soul. Through the darkness and what seemed like fog he saw a man dressed in the habit of a monk, a man dressed in a loose robe, with white hair and beard, and a familiar leather bag hanging over his shoulder. Michael knew instinctively that this was Brother Branislav. Branislav seemed to turn and look directly into Michael's eyes. Michael stared back. Branislav made the sign of the cross, spoke a few words which Michael could not quite hear, and then turned and walked over the hill away from the monastery.

As if hovering above Branislav, Michael watched the monk walk several miles away from the monastery. He did not seem to be in a hurry; as if he already knew his fate was quickly catching up with him. From behind Michael a dust cloud arose. Michael watched as several horses carrying knights quickly caught up with Branislav. They forced him to stop and surrounded him. One knight, a smallish man with brown shoulder length hair and a royal crest on his breastplate came down from his horse. He began talking harshly to the monk. The monk smiled with a look of absolute peace on his face. The knight took his sword and swung at the monk's neck. His head hit the ground with a thud and blood pooled from the severed neck. The knight grabbed the leather bag and rode away. Michael watched as the monk's body slowly deteriorated as the seasons quickly changed. In a matter of moments the body and the head were dust.

A sound startled Michael awake. He lay motionless wishing the unknown to pass by. He was still in a dream like state; barely remembering the dream, yet knowing something had touched the essence of his being. Suddenly something clanged in the hall; he jumped up and almost fell off of the bed. His heart began pounding a million miles an hour. Looking around, he grabbed for the leather bag and held it tightly to his chest. He realized he was hearing the normal sounds of people in the hotel in the morning, doors closing, and voices of other visitors. He glanced at his watch and it was already mid-morning! He had slept for too many hours. He had too much to prepare for. It was time to do something.

Seeing nothing or no one coming through the door, listening carefully for any wayward sounds, and not hearing any, he slowly settled down and lay back on the pillow, still hugging the bag to his chest in a tight embrace, and did nothing.

"I don't know what to do, I don't know anyone in Europe. " Again tears coursed down his cheeks just as they had only a few hours before while he knelt hopeless at the altar. Now the tears were those of fear, dread, darkness and loneliness. Holding the leather bag closely to his chest, he had never felt more alone, emptier, more unprepared for all that this discovery had already brought to him.

Slowly a dim light began forming behind his eyes, the beginning of a thought. Wait a minute, he thought, I do know someone. She has crisp brown hair and those brown eyes of curiosity: Sladjana. He would return to her house with this precious bag and together they would make a plan.

The daylight found Michael driving back into Beograd. He drove directly to Sladjana's apartment, hoping she would be there and somehow understand what was happening with all of this leather bag business and then be willing to help.

He knocked at the door, and she answered with a cup of coffee in her hand. Seeing him, she smiled and quickly invited him inside. He scurried in. He gladly took a coffee and was wondering how to begin to tell her this unbelievable story, or if he even should.

With a sigh, Michael opened his mouth, "I need some help and I don't know anyone else. Some things have happened and I have to tell someone. You're the only one I know. If you have any questions, I will answer them. But I need you to be patient and let me finish what I have to tell you first. I just have to put into words what has happened during the past several hours."

Sladjana now had a very serious look in her eyes as if she was either trying to mimic him or she knew he was very serious.

"I will listen," she said.

Michael seemed frustrated as he ran his hand through his hair. Then he began, "So, I left town yesterday morning....God was it only *yesterday*? Anyway, I was driving sort of South looking for some older monasteries to perhaps do research in. I looked over the side of a hill and saw a series of dilapidated buildings that looked like a monastery. I drove over a bit of a rough cattle trail and parked my car. I realized the construction was about 13th century and there seemed like there had been no repairs."

42

He paused and then turned to look through her window, down onto the street.

"When I looked around, I saw graffiti from Crusaders. They were from the Fourth Crusade, about 1202. Reading their pain, their grief and their lack of direction, tore at my heart. I walked through a small structure and ended up at the altar."

Sladjana's eyes met his and stayed there, as if she were worried about him.

"Look, I felt a little overwhelmed with leaving whatever I had in New Mexico, whatever I had as a teacher searching for whatever I might have had with Julianna, and now I have nothing, okay? Anyway I knelt at the altar. I cried and I prayed. Well as I was lying there I saw a faint outline of an arrow, and I saw that it pointed to the altar. I followed this sign and moved the altar and found a loose stone. I moved the stone and found this leather bag. "Michael held up the strange leather bag as if verifying that what he was telling Sladjana was the truth.

"I looked inside and found a letter from the old Abbot in 1204. He wrote of Crusaders raiding Constantinople and bringing treasures back to his monastery. He wrote of a special cloth," he paused as the wind blew through the cracks in the window and walls, "which was the burial cloth of Jesus Christ. He was overwhelmed. He was also fearful of the cloth being stolen by other Crusaders. So he had a fake shroud made and carried the fake away as a ruse to lead the Crusaders away from the true shroud of Christ. He hid the shroud somewhere. Inside this bag are the letter and a piece of what he calls the shroud."

Sladjana had to interrupt at this point. She could not control the urge any longer.

"And you think it's the *real* cloth?" she asked as if he had lost his mind. However, when she looked at the determined expression in his eyes she understood that he actually believed everything he was telling her.

"Michael," her voice was now a whisper, "are you telling me that you believe you have found the actual linen that wrapped the body of Jesus of Nazareth?" She was in disbelief.

"Sladjana," he spoke calmly but with overwhelming confidence, the look in his eyes very intense now, "It *glows*! Something inside this bag glows."

Michael delicately removed the letter from the bag and Sladjana gasped. She almost dropped her coffee cup but caught hold of herself and placed it on the side table. Michael read the letter to her as tears formed behind her eyes.

When he finished his explanation, Michael looked into her eyes, "Sladjana, I am very scared. I do not know why. No one seems to be after me. No one has threatened me, at least not yet. But, I know this knowledge has caused the death of at least one good man, Abbot Branislav, and I am very frightened it will bring more deaths. There are many men who would *kill* for this. There are many men who *will* kill for this. It's more than a fucking relic! This cloth is a gateway to *divinity*. It cannot fall into the wrong hands, I don't know what I am going to do but I *do* know that I can't let that happen. "

Sladjana was now frustrated and pacing the room, clenching and unclenching her hands as if she didn't know what to do next. In the middle of her stride Michael grabbed her and held her arms so that she was forced to look at him while he spoke.

"There is no one I can trust. There is nobody I can talk to. I don't know what to do, what to say, or where to go, and I am not completely convinced I can trust you either. I came here because you seemed nice enough, you seemed like you cared, and you *did* invite me in for a coffee the other night. "Here Michael breaks the tension with a smile. "*And* I had nowhere else to go."

Michael sat down on the sofa and put his hands to his head. The weight of the universe was on his shoulders and he knew that now he had his own cross to bear.

Sladjana reached across the sofa and grasped his hand, "Michael, my dear. You *can* trust me. And I know that you do or you would not have come here. That is so profound in this day. Thank you. I will help you, although I really do not know what to do or say either. What I believe you need right now is a good sleep. Why don't you lie down on my bed and rest?"

Michael looked at her, his eyelids drooping. He crawled to her bed and was almost asleep as his head hit the pillow.

Sladjana looked at him and let out a sigh before a smile settled across her lips. She pulled a blanket out of her closet, and spread it over him. As she began to walk away, she hesitated, and then turned to look at him. She started walking again, back to the bed where he slept. She crawled under the blanket and pressed her body against him; snuggling up to him and the leather bag that he clung to even in his sleep.

"Don't worry Michael," she whispered, "You can trust *me.*"

Chapter 6

Half way through his Sunday morning sermon, Brother Bob looked up from his notes on the pulpit, past the teleprompter, and into the vast auditorium. His elongated pause and stare caused others to stop what they were doing and look towards the center of the large church. Even those who had been watching this pastor on TV stopped in their tracks and turned their eyes towards their screens and listened. Brother Bob seemed to be readying himself to declare something dramatic. After all, *drama* was his specialty.

He looked around and a feeling of warmth and satisfaction came upon him. He was indeed the voice of God. He knew that God spoke through him in times like this. The prickling of the hairs on the back of his neck was always a sign. And now, at this very moment, was one of the times when he would open his mouth; and it would indeed be the voice, thoughts and ideas of Almighty God that would echo through the walls of the church and out of the speakers of millions of television sets.

Brother Bob looked out over his vast congregation, and then into the camera with the red light on, the one directly in front of the pulpit. He formulated the thoughts gathering in his heart and brain. He opened his mouth, knowing that God Himself was speaking through him. He was the bridge between this world and eternity.

"God has indeed seen the sin of this nation. He is not pleased! He created this nation as a light on the hill and you, YOU" here, Brother Bob pointed at various points of the auditorium and then directly at the camera. "YOU are the guilty one. YOU have allowed sin to settle in this nation, in YOUR community, in YOUR home, and IN YOUR HEART! YOU have not spoken up! YOU have not turned off the sex and the violence on the TV! YOU have not thrown out the books and magazines! And YOU have not turned off the computer. God is not pleased. You have voted and supported men and women who choose death and liberal tendencies rather than the ways of the Bible and life! You have not voiced the outrage of God against the sins of abortion, homosexuality and aggression against democracy. "

At this point Brother Bob began pacing back and forth in front of the podium, while pointing his index finger toward the heavens.

"He is looking from His throne in Heaven and is ready to return to this earth. It is time. Now is the time. We have been talking about this time for thousands of years. But listen to me now, and listen well! NOW is the time. These are *the* last days. Let me tell you this: Before I die Jesus Christ Himself will return to the earth to reign in power. I do not speak lightly and I do not speak flippantly. I know the implications of what I say. I am 45 years old. I know the power of this pulpit. But I also know the voice of God. And HE is speaking through me this morning. NOW, God is readying all of eternity and NOW He is readying His return to the earth."

There was a gasp from the audience followed by a wave of people saying "Amen" in agreement to what their teacher was telling them.

"Get your houses in order. Remove the sin from your homes, your community and this nation. Jesus our Lord will return to this earth in just a few short years. Before I die He will be on the earth. He will judge the living and the dead. He will set all things right. He will establish His Kingdom. And we who are in the right standing with Him will reign over the nations."

Brother Bob looked around. He could see the shock on the faces of his deacons and administrators. This was not in the printed sermon they had worked on this past week. This was not on the website. This message was not prepared and thus they were not going to be prepared for the media frenzy that was to shortly arrive at their doorstep. Oh well, that is why he paid them very good money. They would work overtime to make it all work smoothly.

He had to be the voice of God. And this was indeed God speaking. He knew; he deeply knew that he would not die until he saw Jesus Himself upon the earth again.

The sermon ended. The service ended with wonderful uplifting music, and Brother Bob found himself alone in his office. All the leadership was gathered in the outer office, but no one dared to knock on his door. The voice of the Lord was not to be disturbed unexpectedly.

Bob sat behind his desk and looked up from his King James Version of the Holy Bible and peered into the fireplace. He was alone, except for his dog, Beau, asleep at his feet. Bob knew something had happened in the realms of the world. The unscripted outrage that Brother Bob had expressed that morning in the pulpit did not happen very often. Only a few times in his preaching life had God spoken like that through him and each time it had come to pass. God had begun talking to him many years ago, when he was twelve.

When Bob was a child his father had worked on a ranch owned by a Texas oil tycoon in return for housing for his family. While growing up the son of a poor ranch hand outside of Houston he had almost died when trampled by a mare that had gotten to be a bit out of control. At one point his left lung had collapsed and his heart had stopped beating. He would never forget that during what everyone was certain was the end of his young life, he had left his own body and actually glimpsed into the kingdom of the Lord. That moment was when God began telling Bob what was happening in the world and how the Kingdom of Jesus Christ would be brought into reality through the faithful and complete ministry of Him through Bob. Then the unthinkable happened. His heart started beating again, while in the hospital chapel his own father was on his knees begging to any god that would listen, to save his son. Miraculously, Bob had been sent back to the world of the living, with a purpose. From that day forward, Bob knew he was a Prophet of God and spoke the very essence of the

Word of God in all he did. He actually longed for the day when he would enter God's kingdom again.

Yes, he was a sinner, saved by grace. And who wasn't a sinner? But the Almighty God had selected Bob from the womb to proclaim to the nations His Word and the story of His Son, Jesus, to the world. Bob began small, a simple church in north Houston. But God had blessed him and now, after only 15 years of hard work, prayer and faithfulness, Bob lead the largest mega-church in the entire world: 50,000 people came each and every Lord's Day to worship and hear the word of God. Over 100 million watched him live on TV each Lord's Day. Television was a sinner's tool but through the grace of God, and a nationally syndicated cable network, he was able to bring the word of God to the masses. He had over 1 billion people on his mailing lists. God had indeed blessed him.

Bob had begun a Bible College and Seminary. He had a radio broadcast center that reached around the world. He trained future ministers in his image and sent them forth as his disciples to change the nations.

Bob had met and counseled the past five Presidents. Senators, Congressmen, leaders of Fortune 500 companies, Kings and Prime Ministers called upon Bob for counsel, advice, leadership and prayer. If a political leader went astray, Bob would contact them through email, direct mail, Twitter, and Facebook accounts. Technology was the cause of much sin in this world but Bob had found a way to use it for good. He would contact his followers and force change as God wanted. He kept the leaders walking down the paths of righteousness.

But something had suddenly changed this day. Something stirred within his soul and spirit. Change, *dramatic* change, was in the air. Eternal movement was afoot and Bob was to be a vital part of it all. Brother Bob went to his knees and prayed, listening for the voice of God in his soul. If it were true that he would not die until Christ returned, then it was Bob's mission and duty to bring the return of Christ and thus the rapture of the church to pass. He would be seated at the right hand of Jesus when the unjust and the unholy were sentenced to eternal fire and brimstone.

Several years ago God had given Brother Bob a vision. This vision consisted of knowing that the world and time would come to an end in his lifetime (the book sold 20 million copies and the DVD sold another 50 million!) God told Bob that he would be used as a "prime resource" (that was the exact phrase God had used!) in bringing about the Second Coming of the Lord Jesus Christ. After the vision Bob lay prostrate for two days as the message soaked into his soul. From when he arose, he was a new man and refocused all the energies and resources of this powerful, but humble ministry to the one divine purpose of bringing back the Lord Jesus in this lifetime. Now God had spoken through him in the pulpit to further this particular prophesy. It seemed God was moving even faster than Brother Bob had anticipated, to end time as all knew it, and to bring in the very Kingdom of Heaven.

He pushed his Congressional connections to give billions of dollars more to the development, aid and safety of Israel. He forced the state and national legislatures to enact laws against the perverted homosexual lifestyle. His followers invaded gay bars and burned them to the ground, shot the gay pastors because in reality could one really be a gay pastor? That is absolutely against God's ways! His disciples also burned the metropolitan gay churches in most major cities.

He used these same resources to ensure that absolutely no abortions were ever performed in this country again. Of course, several doctors had died, but at least they were no longer killing unborn babies. The unborn were innocent and the unborn had committed no sin.

He also used this influence to ensure men and some women were elected to local, state and national office who believed in the ways of God. Thus, Brother Bob, and thus God Himself, had his hand in all areas so laws could be enacted, social constraints would be enforced and lives would be changed to glorify the ways of God.

He used his influence to gather other pastors and denominations into his fold providing conservative, that is *biblical*, leadership and action. His billions of dollars in resources sealed the deal for most pastors as they joined his group. He was now, after years of diligent work, the undisputed leader of the Evangelical conservative church in America and throughout the world. No one, absolutely no one, would dare stand against him and His God.

Brother Bob arose from his knees. He called his assistant in and told him to begin a worldwide search of any changes in religious standings and workings from around the globe. Bob then went to bed. He could rest in the faithfulness and goodness of God to carry out His plans for the world.

Now this assistant was not a secretary or coffee getter; Brian Sharp was an expert in getting things done. Karl Rove, the great mastermind behind a recent President was Brian's role-model, hero and mentor. Whatever his boss wanted done; whether legal or otherwise, whether following God, *but wait, whatever his boss wanted was indeed from God*, would be done.

Brian had organized and established a broad reaching process to search out and detect any potential threat to his boss and to the Kingdom of God anywhere in the world. He could reach into most personal computers, even state and corporate owned systems. The monthly newsletters shipped from the church via email and website not only contained news from God and Bob, but also cookies that embedded in the computers and grew backdoors. Through these backdoors Brian and his team could reach in and inquire about most documents and programs in these billions of computers.

The boss had declared something was "happening" somewhere in the world. It was up to Brain Sharp to discover what this "happening" was and how it might affect Bob, the Church, and thus the Kingdom of God.

His team began to search in the various computers and data bases around the world. They searched to inquire if there was any unusual search activity or traffic in the social networks. The search would continue for days until something turned up or Bob and his "feeling" were proven wrong. But Bob was never wrong. Bob had not been wrong since he was twelve years old.

The liberal media had a field day with this sermon from Brother Bob. The commentator spoke over the video of Bob preaching from the pulpit. The voice of the young woman spoke in such a tone as to present Bob as a lunatic who was listening to voices inside his head. Her task was to present this religious person as a person on the edge, which was not really in touch with mainstream America.

Brian noted her commentary and then began a deep search of this woman and her life. He discovered facts and issues in her past life, especially from her college days, and created a file. He then sent this file anonymously to the woman's CNN email address and also to the email of several other prominent news people. Within two days the journalist had killed herself. The issues of her past were too intense and embarrassing for her to keep her job. The other news people learned that if they spoke against Brother Bob, they too would be sent embarrassing emails, complete with any skeletons they may have thought were long gone and turned to dust.

Chapter 7

Michael awoke with a start. The only sound he could hear was the sound of his own heartbeat pounding, out of control, in his head. His breath came in gasps, almost as if he were drowning in a dark place, completely alone. He could feel his insides being shaken apart as if he were the lone victim of a violent storm, ripping and tearing through its path of devastation and tragedy. He happened to be the only obstacle in that path. His body convulsed with spasms and the sweat coming from his pores washed over him like a rising tide. He felt pain, sorrow, and suffering that was simply unlike anything he had ever known. He closed his eyes to brace himself against the next unseen blow from his enemy. Then there was silence. Michael Reagan was having a panic attack.

It took him several moments to recall where he was. He had seen the ceiling in this room many times, and slowly his surroundings became more familiar although not completely at first. He felt something warm on his chest and looked down to find a woman whose face was masked by her flowing locks of hair. She was breathing deeply, serenely, with that wonderful brown hair almost in his face. Juliana, he thought, and had a brief sigh of relief. He had to look back at her just one more time. This was not Juliana.

Then it all began to come back to him. The monastery, the bag, where was the bag? He began to search frantically for it only to realize it was right here beside him. He remembered the drive to Sladjana's house and the long talk with her about their lives, dreams and former lovers.

Her caring concern and willingness, with tears even! She seemed to truly want to help him.

Now as he made the journey into the land of the living from the subconscious mind he woke to find her in his arms, with her face nuzzled against his bare chest. Life sure was wonderful some mornings, even if it got off to a bumpy start. A faint smile began to make its way across his lips as he watched the sunlight move along the wall and over her body. The curtains did an exceptional job of keeping out most of the light but he was still aware that it was climbing higher into a brand new sky and a brand new day.

As Michael lay there staring at the ceiling, the walls and also at Sladjana's sleeping form, he began to develop a plan.

He remembered the letter. It looked authentic, but *was* it? How would he ever prove it? Could Dr. Vivianni shed some light on this? Had Crusader armies passed through that monastery? And what was the name of that monastery anyway? Was there a Monk named Branislav who was an Abbott in that time period at this monastery? Were there any stories or rumors through the years of relics at the monastery? He had at least a million questions and not so much as one answer.

However, *if* the letter and author somehow *did* prove to be authentic, then what? The letter told of a fake shroud and a real shroud. Was the supposed Shroud of Turin the fake shroud? Michael had never believed the Turin shroud to be the genuine article of fabric that had wrapped the body of Christ, but even he agreed that the supporting evidence was quite compelling. If this was the case then where *was* the real shroud? And then there was the clue: *"a place only a holy man will know."* What did it all mean? The more he thought about it the more it sounded like searching for the Holy Grail, or some other artifact that big budget Hollywood productions were made of.

His mind began to race and he wasn't exactly sure what to do next. He supposed he could comb the university library, question church historians, and search the monastery again…and what about Sladjana? He was certain he wanted her help.

Her body began to stir. She looked up at Michael and gently kissed him fully and passionately on the lips. Michael responded. He finally let go of the leather bag and wrapped his arms around Sladjana and pulled her tightly to him. He looked her directly in the eyes. A look of wanting and intensity did not go unnoticed by her. She responded by moving on top of him and snuggling as close as she could get. They simply could not get close enough to one another. As they kissed, their hands began to explore each other and soon the few articles of clothing between them were being removed.

His arms wrapped all the way around her thin form. He put his hand on the striking curvaceous jawbone that defined her face and forced her to look at him. He wanted her to know that whatever he was feeling at this moment was real. She was unlike anything he had ever known and he realized, at that moment, he never wanted to know another the way he wanted to know her, right here and right now. Regardless of what happened or what secrets he had stumbled upon, this particular moment would be forever frozen into his memory. His eyes never left hers, and as he entered her for the first time emotions rippled through him that he never thought were possible. For the first time in his life he did not care about his own pleasure. He only cared about pleasing her. He thrust in and out of her as he traced his thumb across her mouth, never allowing his gaze to leave her own. She too, had never experienced anything like this. The passion within them compounded exponentially with each passing second. This moment, like the piece of linen that now haunted his every waking and sleeping moment, was timeless. He could feel her pelvic muscles tense. In the heat of their passion she spoke to him.

"Oh God! Michael!" her voice was trembling. She could not take her eyes from his gaze.

He looked at her with a look so intense that for a moment she thought his body had been taken over by a hungry animal.

"What?" His voice had become deep and anxious, never taking his eyes from hers.

Now her voice was different too as he wrapped his arm around her neck, pulling her closer to him.

She responded. "I don't ever want another man touching *me*!"

Those words drove him over the edge and to the brink of ecstasy, and he did not go there alone. He took Sladjana on every step of this journey until the two of them were completely spent.

As they lay next to each other, their bodies naked and still holding each other tightly, Michael looked into her eyes and thanked her for last night, the caring and compassion she had shown to him, and also for this morning: ALL unexpected. She smiled and kissed him again. Then she got up, grabbed his shirt and pulled it over her naked body. She walked out and he heard her banging around in the kitchen. Soon he could smell coffee. She brought in two cups, giving him one. She snuggled close to him again under the covers. They could not get enough of each other.

"Well, what is our plan?"

Michael stared at the ceiling as if he had not heard her.

She asked again.

He smiled and told her how he had many things to do and had wanted her to be involved but did not know how to ask her.

"Well," she said, "There are *some* things you certainly have no problem asking for! So I suppose you will be able to ask me to help you on this *history* problem."

He sipped his coffee with a smile and managed to cast continual glances in her direction. She was looking at him as well. She liked the way he pushed his brown hair back from his face when his thought process overpowered his reason.

He told her what he had been planning before he was taken aback with her initial kiss some hours ago. He had to discover if the monastery was active around 1200 A.D. He had to discover if there was an Abbot there at that time period named Branislav. He had to discover if relics or stories of relics had passed through this area in the Fourth Crusade. He *had* to find out if stories were told of a fake shroud. He had to cover a tremendous amount of ground with all of the reading, researching and just talking to people.

Sladjana reminded Michael that she was an IT specialist and therefore could access *the* most important museum and university computers from her laptop. With only a few clicks of her fingers, she could find information, find where to find information, and find necessary people to help solve this problem.

They settled on a plan of action. She would do several searches on her computer. Michael would travel downtown to the museums and libraries and try to talk to people about stories and rumors of the shroud, the monastery, and any hidden letters that may have survived the Crusades.

They would each work hard and meet for dinner. Michael arose out of bed and began cleaning up in the bathroom. Sladjana booted up her laptop and began some searches. She also carefully made a copy of the letter while Michael was in the shower. She hid this copy in a bottom drawer of her dresser under some old books.

Michael walked into the bedroom already dressed. Sladjana, still in his other shirt, stood and began to kiss him goodbye. Michael drew her close, feeling her body against him. Sladjana pushed him away and told him to go downtown to read. She had work to do of her own.

With another kiss, Michael walked out the door. Sladjana turned to her laptop and began to explore various search engines. Both hoped no one might be watching. Both wanted answers. Both hoped light might come to this darkness that was deep inside the leather bag.

Chapter 8

Michael entered the largest Serbian Orthodox church in the city. He was here for a meeting with the Metropolis Pavel; who was the lead pastor of the church. He had hoped that this man who knew the history of the Orthodox Church in Serbia would be able to shed some light and insight into all that had happened during the past few days. It seemed to Michael that at this point he needed a pastor's touch in his life, for his spirit and soul were more confused now than they had been for some time. A few days ago he had been a world away in the confines of a cubicle surrounded by books he never wanted to read. Now he thought he may have been better off to be back there living under the scrutiny of Dr. Vivianni.

He had already spent quite some time at the city library and the university library. It had been a very full and busy day. He only had time to grab a coffee as he walked tirelessly down the road to other appointments. Michael walked into the church, removed his hat, and organized what he wanted to know in his head, before walking up the aisle toward the altar. It was similar in many ways to the altar in the monastery. He began to consider how a *"holy man"* would act and where such a man would look. Michael rested and reflected while he sat in the pew in this quiet, dark church. He blended like a chameleon into the shadows formed by the dim light. Sitting in the quiet darkness he considered what he had discovered already today.

He had managed to confirm that the monastery was indeed named after Saint Prochorus, which explained why the buildings were not on any map. The bigger monastery named for the Saint, which lay a few miles north, had become the focal point of tourists and researchers. Somehow he had stumbled upon the seemingly important place. Several texts in the main library at the University of Belgrade had confirmed the precise location of this monastery and the dates that it had been built. Construction in the mid 1100's would make it an established order as the Crusaders came through in 1204.

As Michael studied maps and diaries of the travels of the soldiers and armies of the Fourth Crusade, he also discovered that some, though not all of the armies had traversed the route around this particular monastery. He had called Sladjana to research more on the particular routes; she was going to get into the Vatican research library for the maps and diaries that were stored there for this precise information. "Beautiful" and "dangerous" were the two words he began quickly associating with her when she came to mind.

Perhaps there had been treasures taken by the army. No one was sure, at least so far; however there were rumors. This was the very reason he wanted to talk to the Metropolis, if and when he showed up. Michael was beginning to wonder if he had come here for nothing. He looked around the dark church and could see no one, so he continued his thoughts. He continued to drive himself to the edge of his own sanity. His thoughts were now coming in waves once again.

There had been a man called "Prince Phillip" in the army. But there was no one of the royal bloodline named Phillip that would have been at this Crusade. Several texts had confirmed that a "Prince Philip" had led part of the crusading army to the battlefield. He was a minor prince from a royal household in what would eventually become France. The stories end with his leadership in battle. There seemed to be nothing of him after the battle and his lineage also seemed to end there. There was also nothing on an Abbot or even a monk named Branislav in that time period. Although there was no complete listing of the abbots of the monastery, there was not a single list that had this name on it. Strange; for if this man was the first or second abbot, one would assume his name would be somewhere. All things considered it had been a pretty good day for the first day. Now to find this man and hear what he knew. If in fact he was here to find.

Just as he gave up on finding the Metropolis and rose to leave in frustration Michael noticed a monk, a priest; in holy garb before the altar who was bowing face down. The man slowly and deliberately lifted his head up towards heaven as if in prayer. As a seemingly otherworldly light seemed to fall upon his face, Michael realized his lips were moving without making a sound.

Michael cleared his throat for no other purpose than to make his presence known. He did not know the description of the man whom he was supposed to see. So he waited. Eventually the praying priest bowed again, and arose from his knees. He stood looking at the cross. Then he turned and smiled at Michael.

He introduced himself as Pavel, Metropolis of all the Church in Beograd. He shook Michael's hand warmly and invited him to the back of the church for a more comfortable place to sit. They sat with a small Turkish coffee. The aroma of ground beans, cardamom and the intensity of it all in the small cup overwhelmed Michael with memories, feelings, places and events where he had drank such coffee and lived wonderful parts of his life. Pavel peered into Michael's eyes so long that Michael turned away in embarrassment.

Michael knew that this holy man could see the sin, doubt, disturbances, and waywardness of his soul and the wrongness of his life. He saw straight through him and most likely already knew which direction his soul was headed. Most likely it was a downward spiral into the pits of darkness and eternal damnation that would someday consume him. Finally, Pavel sipped his coffee and began to speak.

"I sense darkness in you." The old man's smile faded quickly into an expression of undeniable concern. "You have come a long way to find a connection to your life. Why don't you tell me your story and let us see if we can help each other."

Michael, not knowing what else to say, began to tell him his story. He felt compelled to tell him everything. It seemed as if this holy man already knew these things, and

Michael was just pouring out his very soul and life to him. Once he began he could not stop. He talked about leaving New Mexico, the flight, the loss of Julianna, and meeting Sladjana. He told the man about finding the monastery and crying and praying at the altar. He spoke of the arrow and then the letter. All the time Pavel sat, patiently sipping his coffee and watching Michael. There were no other sounds or movements. Finally, when Michael finished, exhausted and relieved, there were several minutes of silence.

Darkness crept into the room; as the fire on the grate grew smaller. Michael sat with his head in his hands and hoped for some miracle that would help him in this moment.

Finally, after long moments, Pavel spoke. In a deep, soothing voice that could have been twenty years younger, he began to tell a story.

"When I was a young novice an old priest befriended me. He was nearly 100 years old. He told me stories of the past."

"What kind of stories?"Michael asked, as if he were too impatient to wait for the answers he so desperately wanted.

"Patience my son, you will get the answers you seek."

Although the Metropolitan was a soft spoken man of God, Michael could tell he was not a man to be pushed, and allowed him to continue without interruption.

"Stories of our religion, of the church in Serbia, of great men in monasteries around the kingdom. This old man looked into my eyes and told me that I was the *true* keeper of the history of Christ in Serbia. These stories have been passed down from priest to priest for centuries. He told me that one day a man would come to me with a story and a letter. I have waited my *entire life*. I question myself, are *you* this man? I look into your eyes now and wonder if I see your true soul. Can I *trust* you with the stories I was entrusted with? I sat here listening to your story, to your voice, to your very *spirit* as you told me about yourself, and what you have found. You have trusted me with much and I am grateful. I do believe that I can trust you with what I know."

Michael took a deep breath. He now wondered if the answers he so desperately sought were the answers he even wanted to hear. He sensed danger ahead, but did not interrupt Pavel.

"There was a man many years ago who was given a gift. Yes, he was Abbot Branislav. You cannot find him in any histories, because we have hidden him. We did not want others to know about the gift. But he was the first and really, the only Abbot of the monastery you found. We have left those buildings in disrepair so people would not look at them but at the big, public monastery further up the road. But you, my son, found it all. You found the buildings, you found the arrow, and you found the letter. We were told not to look for clues, but to wait with our stories and another would come with the evidence. So we waited for eight centuries, now you have come.

Abbot Branislav walked away from the monastery on that fateful morning knowing he would never return. He had in his bag a letter and the false shroud. His goal was to get far away from the real shroud and to see what God would do for him. He walked for three days, always going west. Finally in the afternoon of the fourth day, the Crusaders caught him and took him prisoner. They tortured him to make him talk about the treasures and the shroud. Surely God helped him, for he told only the lie. He never spoke of the monastery or the real shroud. The Crusaders seemed to believe him. They looked in the bag he carried and found the cloth with the stain of the human form on it. You know this as the Shroud of Turin. They bowed in prayer and worship as they realized this was the form of Christ. They also knew that they could sell this and make much money for them and their families.

The Crusaders kept Branislav tied up for two days as they planned what to do with the Shroud they had found. Their plan was to kill the abbot and then take the cloth to the Vatican. After the plan was agreed to, the men drank, ate and then fell asleep. One of the men, a knight, killed the other three knights while they slept. He then killed the abbot. He placed their bodies in a nearby cave. He took the shroud, the letter, and the other treasures the knights had collected, then rode west back toward his home.

This is the story told to the priests through the centuries. We knew what happened because a novice monk had followed Branislav and watched to see how God would deliver the Abbot and the shroud. But God did not deliver anyone or anything. The novice returned to the monastery and told this story to all the monks. They wept, they tore their robes, and they walked away from the monastery never to return.

But the novice kept this story and told a novice when he had grown quite old. That novice told another and eventually I was told. Now I tell you. That is the story."

All this time Michael had held his head in his hands. But as the story unfolded, a light had grown in his heart. He knew he was being told the truth. He knew he was a continuation of this lineage of men who had known this story. He also knew he was perhaps the end of the line.

"What about the real shroud in the monastery? What became of that?" Michael asked sheepishly.

The Metropolitan placed a steady stare on Michael's face. He stared for some minutes as Michael waited. Michael's own gaze never wavered from the man. He needed answers. Finally, Pavel opened his mouth, tried to say something, and closed it again. He did this a few times until finally he found his voice.

"We do not know. No one knows what happened to the real shroud. Branislav told no one what he did with it. We always assumed it was somewhere in the monastery, but no one could find it. So, over time, we gave up the task and waited for God to work. It seems now God has worked, and brought *you* to us."

"So what do I do now? I'm not a detective. I am only a teacher and sometimes a researcher, and *most* of the time I wonder about that. What *DO* I do now? And, *if* I found the Shroud, what happens then? Really, what am I to do then? And who will believe that what I find is the *real* shroud versus the Shroud of Turin? I am in quite a predicament don't you think? I 'm damned if I move forward and I cannot remain where I am. What do I do, Father? Just tell me what I am supposed to do!"

The priest looked down at the confused face of Michael. He did not know what to do. He was more of a politician than a man of the spirit. But he still knew God's hands were in these events. He could see how God was moving to open doors, and to bring the events of 900 years ago to their fulfillment, now. He did not know how it all would end, but he *did* know God was involved.

The priest stood before Michael, laid his hand on his bowed head, made the sign of the cross, turned and walked away. Michael watched the priest walk back to the main altar, bow before it and peer up to the feet of Jesus.

Alone again, he was now convinced he was on the verge of a nervous breakdown. Whereas only a few days ago he was behind his desk at the university, swallowed by dust, now he was sitting in a church being told a story that could not possibly be true, even though it certainly *felt* like the truth he had been hearing. If all of these things *were* to be true, then history was on the verge of being changed. If it were *true*, he was teetering on the edge of darkness with this truth. *If it were true*; but it could not be true. Michael had spent too many years in academic research to believe that dreams and folklore would ever be trusted so deeply as to change history.

The pressure was building in his head and heart. Confusion reigned and his mind switched back and forth from the dream, the stories, the bag and the document. It all opposed *documented* history, the *truth* as has been known for hundreds of years, and all of academic research for 500 years. Nothing he had heard in these past two days could go against this. Yet, at the same time pressure was building deep in his heart, a light was dawning there too. What *if* he had been taught *lies* and the truth was just told to him by this old holy man?

Michael walked the darkening streets back to Sladjana's place. His mind switched quickly and painfully between the two worlds: academic research and the stories and dreams. Which to trust? Which was right? *Why am I even listening to dreams?* He could come to no clear settled state of mind before he walked into her doorway and could find a way to tell Sladjana what he had learned.

While Michael was away all day, Sladjana had been busy on her computer and the internet. She was researching all aspects of the Shroud of Turin and any other shrouds that might have turned up through the centuries. She was also trying to discern if any relics of medieval churches might have been called shrouds or pieces of shrouds.

She had been going between scores of university and church libraries which included the Vatican. Just because she was a nice girl did not preclude her from using her computer skills to hack into places some people might not have wanted her to look. She looked, took notes, and learned much. She did manage to find old maps of the travels of the Fourth Crusade. She discovered stories of relics found and taken from Constantinople, and finally she ran across a story written by a monk about an abbot that had been killed. She would keep this information close, to share with Michael over dinner.

When she got the phone call from Michael about searching deeper into the libraries at the Vatican, she opened another computer, and dedicated that computer to research the Vatican. She began searching specifically for diaries and maps of the Fourth Crusade, and then narrowed the search to maps and diaries of Crusaders in Serbia in 1204. After searching for over an hour, this computer finally buzzed that something interesting had been found. A diary of a knight had surfaced. It had been written on his deathbed in 1231. It seems the knight had asked a monk to write the story of his life. He had fought in the Fourth Crusade and had found his way back, with three other knights, to a certain monastery to rest. Sladjana paused and downloaded the entire entry. Just as she did, her computer connections all over the house, including her cell phone were cut off. She thought this was strange, but thought that lightning had perhaps hit a cell tower somewhere in the distance. Damn storms.

Sladjana was ready to get up anyway and begin getting ready to meet Michael for dinner. But the timing of the lost connections still bothered her, and lingered in the back of her mind.

Chapter 9

Brian Sharp paced back and forth across the room that served as a command center for Brother Bob's quest. His name could not have been more appropriate because he was indeed a *very* intelligent man. He had spent many years of his life heading military black ops teams and was an expert at finding information that was never supposed to be found. He had seen the madness of war from a dangerously close perspective. He had tortured and he had killed in his former life all in the name of the United States Government, and for the sake of protecting his country. He walked with a purpose. He was proud of his life and the horrors he had survived. He was yet to meet a man that he feared, even at forty two. Brian Sharp was a patriot and a hero, at least to Brian Sharp.

After leaving the United States Marine Corps at thirty years old, Brian had decided that the rest of his life would be spent somehow defending the greater good for all of mankind, so he went back to school. Soon after graduating he had heard Brother Bob speak for the first time, and he was genuinely moved by the things this man had talked about. Brother Bob was an extraordinary voice for the righteous. And if Bob was the voice then Brian Sharp was the right arm. He went to work for Brother Bob soon after hearing him speak and it didn't take long for Bob to notice the fire and loyalty that lay in the man's heart. Bob liked him and now he was Bob's right hand man. Nothing usually got to Brother Bob without first making it past Brian Sharp.

Now Brian stood still in the command center, dressed in a tailored suit that made him appear to be FBI. He had his team using software to search constantly on the internet for anyone that appeared to be doing specific religious research. Nothing had turned up for several hours until a person was discovered in China doing unusual research on the original documents of the Bible. This caused Brian to see red flags. If the Bible were to be disproven in any way, this could hurt the ministry and the Kingdom of God. Brian dispatched several key members of the team to keep an eye on this research and determine more precisely what was happening.

Another computer in North Carolina was doing deep and extensive research on Creationism versus Evolution. This research was way beyond any normal academic paper. This person had downloaded too much information that perhaps could hurt the work of God. Brian knew that no matter how much academic writing and research scientists found that further proved the age of the earth, the fossil collection continuing to show a long pathway from when the earth came to be and the very short time mankind had been on the soil, and even evidence of the evolution of humans, this research could never be shown to the public for it would take away from the basic belief that God created the earth and He was in total control of humanity. Another team was sectioned off to keep their eyes on this computer.

It was amazing to Brian how so many people thought what they were doing on their home computers would never be seen. No one was protected from searching eyes. Every computer linked in any way to the internet was open for perusal and knowledge. Brian and his team kept their eyes on everyone and then more. God was looking right into their hard drives and they didn't even give it a thought. These ignorant masses of people trusted the government and private phone companies and the puny firewalls and virus protections on their computers to protect them from any intrusion. If these masses really cared to know, they would be frightened to know that everything is known, and nothing is hidden from the government, private organizations, and the marketing companies of Wall Street.

All over the world people researched things on religion. Sometimes Brian's people would make sure websites could not be visited, ensuring that they could keep some ideas from the searching public. At other times, these Christian computer geeks would make sure only the websites they wanted you to see and know about would come up in the searches. All things were possible with those who knew what to do.

Brian had grown up steeped in the fundamentalist ideas of Christianity. He believed in God from a young age, and had a strong and firm commitment to the things of God, as outlined in the King James Version of the Holy Bible. He had been called to the work of the ministry when he was 15 years old and had worked in his church youth group. He even preached on a few occasions.

As Brian got older, not only was he was torn between his strong academics and desire to learn mathematics, computers, and science, but also his desire to serve God. He finally compromised by going from high school to the United States Marine Corps and eventually earned a degree in science at Liberty College, the birthplace of the Falwell conservative movement, courtesy of God and his G.I. Bill. Brian believed that becoming grounded in the ways of God and the Bible as an adult would strengthen him as he attended more liberal anti-Christian universities later to earn his advanced science and computer degrees.

While at the Bible College, Brian had fallen in love with a young Christian woman, Dawn. Indeed, the love did dawn between them and also blossom into a commitment. As these two students grew in their relationship, Brian realized that Dawn, who was ten years younger than him, wanted to explore more intimately each other's bodies. Brian had made a commitment to God to save himself in all ways until marriage. Dawn would not give up as her hands explored Brian's body and Brian tried to resist, but his own body, led by Satan, of course, betrayed him.

One night after he and Dawn had walked home from church, they were drinking a cup of hot cocoa in her room. One thing led to another and Satan entered the room. They got naked and lay on the bed. Brian could not help himself. It was as if another had entered his body just before he entered Dawn's body. Afterwards Brian felt totally ashamed and forsaken.

He spent days afterwards not only ignoring Dawn, for she could not be the righteous Christian woman he had been led to believe, but Brian fasted, spent hours in prayer and read ONLY the Bible seeking the forgiveness and grace of God. Only after some months did Brian feel any kind of peace again. But Brian knew that in order to stay on the right path with God, he would need to never be near a woman again. It seemed women brought out sinfulness in him and took him away from the things of God.

After telling her very calmly that she was a godless whore, Brian never saw Dawn again. He did hear that some months later she had dropped out to attend some liberal school. Brian then knew in his heart that Satan had brought Dawn to tempt him away from the path God had made for him. Brian would never lose sight of that path again.

Brian graduated and then was accepted to Massachusetts Institute of Technology (MIT); probably the most prestigious engineering and technological school in the world, to earn advanced degrees in computer technology and programming. Brian felt renewed strength in his faith in God and knew that this next step would lead to the ministry God had eternally planned for him.

While at MIT those six years, there had been another liaison but this time it was with his study partner Joseph, a doctoral student from China. Brian chose never to think about this event and considered it, again, as a massive attack of demons from hell working to destroy his soul. Brian repented with fear, fasting, and living that winter with his window open to punish himself for the easy way he transgressed against the ways of God.

Brian came to realize that any type of sex was forbidden to him. This was the path Satan had chosen to destroy his soul. As long as he kept away from any type of sex, then the ways of God would be open to him. God would smile on him, open doors for him, and all would be good. So he renounced sex of any kind. He refused to watch any movies, did not listen to anything but Christian radio, and did not watch TV *unless* it was about the Bible. Brian was safe to walk the path of God.

He was hired by Brother Bob straight out of university after he had earned his PhD. While Brian could have earned hundreds of thousands of dollars after graduation, he knew God had opened doors to be able to work for this ministry. He was able to use the gifts God had given to him to aid Brother Bob, and thus the Kingdom of God, in reaching the world and preparing it for the Second Coming of Jesus! After all, Brother Bob had said so.

Brian ceased thinking about the ways God had worked in his life and returned his focus to the problem before him. Someone was trying to destroy the Work and Word of God somewhere in the World. God had told these things to Brother Bob. What more could Brian do to place more resources into searching?

Then another flag came up. Someone in Serbia was researching the Shroud of Turin. So many people kept searching on this topic that Brian didn't care anymore. But this person kept digging deeper, searching databases of universities and then hacking into the Vatican! This was *not* good. The intruder was finding documents on subjects even Brother Bob did not know about, also going into the databases of the oldest university libraries, researching relics, ideas of the shroud, and rumors of the shroud. Whoever this person was, they were obviously on a mission and searching for something.

This might be the issue Brother Bob was called upon by God himself to deal with. Brian pulled his best two person team: Warner and Meredith, to look deeply into this matter, and return with a report in 24 hours.

Chapter 10

Michael was already seated at the candlelit table long before Sladjana arrived. It's not as though he purposely arrived early, he just needed a place to have a drink and sit. A place to organize his thoughts on all that had happened during this tremendous day. So he sat alone at a table for two slowly drinking a daiquiri. This was a habit he had picked up while exploring Bourbon Street in New Orleans, now a world away. As he went over facts, stories, and the thoughts of the past several hours, his eyes glazed over and he simply allowed his mind to wonder.

He could not believe this was happening to him. He considered all of the coincidences that had brought him to this table tonight. The argument with Dr. *"what's her name"*, Julianna not being around, his falling into some sort of intense emotional rollercoaster ride with Sladjana, the "discovery" of the monastery, and then the arrow. Too many coincidences were beginning to throw up red flags, and a lot of them. Was someone or something trying to manipulate his life? Was this really happening or was he on a drinking binge soon to wake up like he had so many times, on a side street near Café Monde on the banks of the Mississippi River? Or was this *really* happening, and he was on the verge of something *astounding*? Something that had been gone from this world for over two thousand years, lying in wait, until the time was meant for it to surface. This led Michael to ask himself more questions. Why now? Why *my* lifetime? Why *me*?

He drank a little more and was not aware of the other tables around him. If someone had been looking at him, they would have seen a man simply staring out the window toward the Danube River. But Michael knew deep within his heart that he was walking into strange, unknown, and perhaps *eternal* territory. He was walking a path laid out by *God*, although he really was not a religious man anymore; but his Sunday school upbringing still abruptly raised its head at the worst of times. Those lessons seemed near to him now in this dark place. He knew he was treading on holy ground, and he knew his next steps had to be taken very carefully.

At that moment a shadow fell over him and his view became obstructed. His hazy eyes returned to focus and there she was; a most lovely looking lady, could it be? The long hair, the nice figure, was it really *her*? Michael shook his inner head and moved from dreamy thoughts to stare into the face of Sladjana, *not* Julianna.

"Your mind was a million miles away, my dear. What were you thinking?"

Catching himself before he said anything that he might regret, Michael blurted, "The River, I was looking at the river and dreaming of simply sailing down that river, and forgetting about all of this and everyone here, except for you, of course." He wasn't sure if he had succeeded in catching himself.

Sladjana knew this was a bizarre type of lie, or something, but let it pass. She had too much to talk about and she was starving. It had been a very long day at *work*.

Sladjana ordered a drink, and began to question Michael about his research. He paused to try and collect his thoughts. He began by talking about his research in the Belgrade University libraries, and how he had confirmed the existence of the monastery. He told her of Crusaders from the Fourth Crusade that had come through the area, and of a Prince Phillip, who seemed to have been killed about that time period. Then he told her the story from Pavel, and how this had changed things. As a researcher he knew that oral traditions could hold significant kernels of truth, and were *not* to be taken lightly. So in retelling the story to Sladjana, he could see more areas of truth, and how it *all* seemed to fit with the facts as he seemed to know them now. Michael became even more convinced that they were on the right track toward the real shroud of Jesus, the burial cloth of the single most important human being to ever walk the face of the earth. For a moment he thought he would vomit from fear and uncertainty.

After ordering their meals, Sladjana began telling of her research on the web. She explained how she had hacked into several libraries around the world, including the forbidden, the Vatican. She gave Michael a crooked smile, letting him know that she was very proud of herself, and her abilities. She had discovered maps, diaries, and deathbed confessions of people around that time period.

The one deathbed confession that intrigued her most was of a knight who told of the killing of an abbot. She would show Michael the complete text when they returned home.

And so they ate. They spoke of their lives, their tastes in music, their religious experiences, their failures and successes in relationships. Michael told her of how he once got so tired of people in general, that he got lost in the Blue Ridge Mountains of Virginia, for three weeks. They laughed *with* and *at* each other as they consoled each other. At some point, Michael looked down and they had been holding hands across the table for some time, while they ate their dessert. It was time to leave. Michael; not really knowing where he might spend the night, and feeling sort of apprehensive about it, was relieved when Sladjana invited him back to her place.

"In fact", she stated as she looked at him with a very serious look on her face, "why don't you stay at my place the whole time you're here? That way we can research, and plan together, and try our theories out on each other. And...", she came closer, then grabbed him close to her, and planted a wet kiss on his mouth, feeling his lips with her fingers "we can make love each night!"

Michael lost his breath with her touch.

They walked home. Michael elated all the great prospects in front of him, and beside him, as Sladjana gripped his arm.

The living room floor was littered with printouts and notes. Sladjana had indeed been working hard. In the center of the chaos was a map. Michael looked at it, comparing it to the current road map of where the monastery was in Serbia. Indeed, an army of Crusaders had passed within less than a mile of the monastery. So it was possible some had taken solace and refuge in the buildings and at the altar. He began to smile. He picked up a printout of the diary of a knight; and read it aloud:

"This is the testimony and last confession of Albert, a knight of Sir John Lucius of Rheims. I served my lord John all my life, as my father, and his father has served that household. Now, upon my bed where I shall soon see the face of God, I tell a story and hope to be absolved from my sin.

I traveled with many other knights from this area on what came to be known as the Fourth Crusade, it was the Crusade of Liberation. Though many horrific things happened on that journey, I tell of what I did after we left Constantinople. I left that city laden with treasures of gold, fine linens, parchments and jewels. I rode with three other knights from this realm; we helped each other stay alive, and gain wealth beyond our own imaginations. Our plan was to return home and live in luxury for ourselves and our children.

After we crossed back into the Kingdom of Serbia, we returned to the monastery that sheltered us before we went to war. Something was not right at that place. Doors were left open, when before they were bolted. There was no mass being spoken and the monks were scattering. Dead and dying men and women were all around, remnants from the destruction of Constantinople. I forced a monk to the ground and compelled him, by hacking off two fingers from his right hand, to tell me what was happening. He told me the abbot had left with a treasure of the finest quality. He had stolen it from Prince Phillip, renounced the order, and fled away from the army.

This was not right. So we four pursued him. After two days we caught up with the abbott. He, knowing his time was close, stopped. Bowed in prayer and after again much compelling; he told us how he had left the order to hide his treasure. He had found a cloth and was going to sell it to the highest bidder and live like a king instead of an abbot. We knights were shocked such a holy man would do such a thing. We knew that the cloth was valuable, so we took it from the monk, and tied him up until we decided what to do with him.

We four knights sat around the fire that night after some wine, and talked about what we would do with all the goods we had taken. I discovered these men had many more valuables than I did. Jealousy and greed raged within me. I waited until they were all asleep. I then slew each of the three knights with my sword. The abbot, fearing for his life, began to pray. I walked to the tree where we had tied him and thrust my sword through his heart, basking in pleasure, at the destruction of this man's life.

I gathered all the goods including the valuable cloth from the abbot. I rode away, leaving my sin, and entered the darkness of my soul. As I rode along, I knew God would bring destruction and death upon my household. I vowed to give Him my gifts. When I entered the village of Turin in Italy, I placed the cloth upon the altar, and walked away.

I have kept these things hidden within my soul for too many years. I now desire to get them out and be forgiven, if possible, before I shall soon stand before God, who will certainly send my soul into the abyss. At least I can beg."

Michael and Sladjana locked eyes. This was the same story, but from a different angle, that Pavel had told. All was being confirmed. The authentic shroud that wrapped the earthly body of Jesus Christ was still in the monastery. But where? Neither Michael nor Sladjana could determine "where only a holy man would look".

Sladjana broke into Michael's reverie, and told him how all of her internet connections had suddenly stopped working, just when she downloaded this diary fragment. She was not too concerned, but still this bothered her; as if someone had pulled her plug. Michael was becoming more paranoid as the entire story unfolded. He had seen nothing yet; but he had read too many spy novels not to be suspicious. He was convinced that someone was watching, and this bothered him.

It was getting late. The wine was settling into their brains as well as their bloodstreams. They both got up and walked back to Sladjana's room. As Michael got ready for bed, he quietly tried to digest and understand the significance of all they had found. He lay in bed when Sladjana came into the bedroom, completely naked, pausing in the doorway as her figure was silhouetted in the dim light, her hair flowing down her back. She lay down beside him, to find him already asleep. Disappointed, she pulled on a nightshirt, and waited to follow him into sub-consciousness.

Michael was dreaming, and it was quickly turning into a nightmare. At first he could feel himself moving, above a barren landscape, effortlessly, as if every known law of physics were under his complete control. He was climbing higher into the clouds, before the soft white waves scattered from beneath him, and he saw the horrors underneath for the first time.

He saw fire, starvation, and death. There were armies gathered beneath him in an epic battle. He could see humanity, he could see goodness, and all that was right, falling off into cracks in the earth. The innocent cried out, and the innocent were destroyed, swallowed by the lava that flowed from the cracks. He had a bird's eye view of the horrors beneath him, but he could do nothing to stop any of it. Just when he closed his eyes to block it all out, he was somewhere else.

He was bound, and he was in pain. The pain was so excruciating that he could feel vomit rising in the back of his throat, choking the life out of him. He could not breathe and he could not see. He could hear the sound of a crowd mocking him, and antagonizing him. Although he tried to open his eyes against the crashing pain in his face, all he could see was the red flow of blood blocking his vision. His body convulsed and he could not feel his arms and legs. He raised his head to the heavens to beg God for mercy, but God was nowhere to be found. Then he was above the clouds again, witnessing his own execution. While he watched he could feel his own flesh being ripped apart. There was absolutely nothing he could do. Then he awoke.

Warner and Meredith were ex-Marines that had known each other for too many years. They first met in Iraq, and had been on several missions together around Baghdad, and close to the borders of Iran. They had each saved the life of the other on more than one occasion. They had grown as brothers in arms and brothers in life.

When they returned home to Jacksonville, NC to Camp Lejeune between tours, these two men began hearing rumors of Omega. This private organization was offering good money for seasoned soldiers who were experienced in providing personal protection in war zones. Warner and Meredith talked about the possibility of leaving the Marines and joining Omega. They decided to meet with a representative in New Bern, which was located only a few miles from the Omega campus.

On a Saturday afternoon in early December, with all of the town's Christmas decorations in place, the two Marines met in room 512 in the Hilton Hotel with Ben Green. While overlooking the Trent River and the sailboats rolling in the ripples of the water, Ben told the men about the history of Omega and the present and future missions.

Not looking at the men, but keeping his eyes focused on the Neuse River as it emptied beyond the horizon into the ocean, Ben told the story.

"Our leader, let's call him Henry. He sort of likes that name as it reminds him of King Henry of France, who led a large Crusade to rid the Holy Land of the heretic menace. Well, Henry had a vision from God several years ago that God was going to use America to defeat the forces of Islam. After 9/11, Henry used the influence he had built through the years in the military, with religious organizations, and in the business world, to grow a private army that world work with and also support the American military. The Bush White House totally supported this formula, thus freeing up the Marines and Army to actually work to take out the bad guys.

So for the past few years we have been actively recruiting fellow soldiers and Marines to enter this work, and serve not only their nation, but also God. So, gentlemen, we meet today."

Warner lit a cigarette and broke in with a salient question: "Do we have to be Christians or something to join? I know I really don't believe in much, although I *have* been known to pray when enemy fire starts blowing the shit out of my position."

"No, we trust God to work in each man's heart. What we *want* is a trained soldier, experienced in battle and able to take orders. We trust that as you are around your fellows, and are exposed to the way this organization is run, God *will* work in your heart and things will change.

We offer four times the salary you are now getting in the United States Marine Corps. We offer a bonus of $25,000 every time you fulfill a 6-month contract. We offer full health, dental, optical, and life insurance plans. We contribute 50% of whatever we pay you toward an IRA retirement plan. We ask for obedience, trust in the leadership, and *secrecy* from telling anyone outside of your group. What do you think?"

Warner and Meredith looked out the window and watched as the new Cunningham Bridge stopped traffic; and then lifted its massive two 100,000 pound arms to allow a nice looking 35 foot sailboat to glide into the river, and down toward the ocean. Each was lost in their own thoughts of what they could do with their money after a few years of serving in this new force. They also considered that if they were going to return to Iraq or Afghanistan; why not get paid what the trials and pain were worth, and still serve their country? As for the religion aspect, well, they could keep their religion and take the money.

Meredith looked at Warner; they knew a decision had been made. Meredith looked at Ben. "We like what we hear. We want to join your organization, *but*, we still have one year on our tour of duty with the Corp. Can we get back to you then?"

"Of course I know you are committed to Uncle Sam for another year. I did not expect you to join today. But I want you to consider this offer open-ended. When you return from your next tour in Afghanistan, come see me." He handed both men his card with just his name, "Ben", and a cell phone number. "I believe we can work well together. And, when you are in Kabul or those surrounding areas later this year, stop by and talk to our men, learn from them. They will know we have had this conversation, and they will be happy to share how they feel about Omega with you."

With that the men shook hands, and Ben walked out of the room. Warner and Meredith continued watching the boats for a while. Meredith smiled to himself while thinking of his new salary. Then they stood and also walked out of the room.

That meeting had happened over three years ago. The two men did serve another year in Afghanistan, where they met some of the guys from Omega. They had drinks, told stories, and discovered Omega guys were just like them. Both Warner and Meredith felt comfortable around these guys, and felt they could be part of the team. They returned home and joined the organization. It was as interesting and full of money as they had suspected. After serving two years with Omega, and realizing that perhaps the ways of God were good, these two *brothers* began looking around for more opportunities to serve the Lord Jesus, and also earn more money with their expertise.

Warner and Meredith, the two seasoned soldiers who spent too many tours in Iraq and Afghanistan with the United States Marines, went on to spend several more tours all over the world providing personal protection with Omega. They had each also earned a Master's degree in computer science. They had come to Brother Bob and his ministry as a team. They had not only served together, but had grown together as an inseparable force to be reckoned with in the trenches of warfare. They had been saved while working with Omega, and felt the call of God on their lives to serve his Kingdom, and to protect the work of God around the world.

These two men were experienced in warfare of all kinds, and were willing to sacrifice their lives, not only for their country, but for the Kingdom of God. They were ready to die, or help others die; to protect what they believed was right, true, and necessary. These men had been assigned the task of finding Sladjana and Michael.

Chapter 11

Michael awoke with a start. He knew where the Shroud was! Somehow he knew where only a holy man would look. *He knew!* This was awkward to say the least. He looked across the bed at the sleeping form of Sladjana and realized that, if anything, he was *not* a holy man. But still he knew. *Where would a holy man look?* He would be bowing at the altar and looking up to the crucified form of Jesus on the cross. He had seen the priests and even Pavel do this in the church. He himself had done this at the monastery, just before he found the leather bag.

Michael lay in bed. His arms were behind his head. He was fully awake now and thinking at the speed of sound. He would have to return to the monastery and do a thorough search behind the altar. He would have to discover what had happened to the crucifix that hung behind the altar 700 years ago. He would have to work. He was excited now and found it difficult to just lie there.

Sladjana stirred and turned over on her pillow to face him. She squinted open her eyes and a half smile crinkled her mouth. She drew closer to Michael, pressing herself comfortably against him, and went back to sleep. Michael loved the touch of this wonderful woman. Her warmth, her intelligence, her sexuality, and her obvious affection for him aroused him anew this early morning. It was four a.m.

Michael had to get up even though it was still the middle of the night. The researcher part of his brain was moving too quickly to just lie there. He had to sit, he had to write, and get all that he knew down on paper. He sat at the laptop, her laptop, and began to document all that had happened to him. He tried to approach the story as a historical document instead of the love story it was quickly becoming. Dispassionately, he began to write. With every keystroke he could see the document coming together. This would be his dissertation. This *could* be several articles that would finally get him published in reputable journals. He could have a stronger resume, and apply to better universities. *This* could be the cover of *TIME* magazine. This was the story he had been waiting for. He had found *the original* shroud of Jesus. Every publication known to mankind would want his story. Job offers would pour in. "Dr what's her name" back in New Mexico could go straight to hell, and he would laugh and smile, as she descended into the pit.

It took two hours before Michael had what he wanted written and documented. He could see several gaps that would need to be filled, but this would come with more research and interviews. But he had the story of the millennium. He knew where the Shroud was located. Now he had to get it. But then what? Who could he trust with such a......he didn't know what to call it; A piece of history? It was definitely more than a religious artifact. It was an icon, and much more than just an idol to worship as well. Whatever it was, he needed a plan.

He heard Sladjana move around in the bed. He was suddenly very tired. He needed more sleep. Michael slipped back between the sheets, pulled the blanket up to his chin and curled up next to this sleeping woman who had grasped his heart. With her back to him, he wrapped his arms tightly around her and held her. Once this discovery was complete, he could give them both a new life.

The charter plane landed while Michael was having breakfast. Warner and Meredith gathered their gear and exited the plane, flashing their diplomatic credentials at the Serbian officials. A car was waiting for them. They were driven directly to the street where the computer was still linked to the internet. The two men sat at the café on the corner, and drank cups of coffee while Brian made his decisions. Being in constant communication with Brian back in Houston was a strong benefit. He gave real time data on what was happening. In fact, he had accessed the laptop camera, and was looking live into the room where the computer was sitting, admiring Sladjana's naked torso.

Sladjana's laptop was turned on and open. This made things so much easier for Brian. He accessed all the internet searches done recently. As he peered into the living room he also listened to any sounds coming from inside the house. He was connected. As he was trying to see what the camera was seeing he opened the documents, one by one, and read. He learned that these people had been searching for information about the Shroud of Turin, and that they were very interested in the history of it. He learned that they were also researching the Fourth Crusade, and the story about a monastery near Belgrade. He learned about Branislav, and the diary in the Vatican.

He got to Michael's recent document and a low whistle blew through his teeth. He now knew he was on the correct track. These were the people Brother Bob had known about, it never ceased to amaze him that Bob was never wrong. He knew what they had found, and were searching for. He actually believed that *they believed* they had found the real shroud of Jesus. Then he paused. If they *had* found the real shroud, what did this mean? How would his life, the life of the ministry, the life of the world change? Had God so worked His divine plan, that He had moved heaven and hell, to place Brother Bob and also Brian at such a time as this? To be involved in the finding of this shroud and all that might happen after? An involuntary shiver rose up Brian's spine. He was dealing with eternal and almighty things here. He needed to call Brother Bob. But not yet, he wanted to sift through more information.

Brian did not know what to make of this information. But he would continue digging, watching, and listening. Several hours passed and then a figure approached the laptop. It was a man with messy hair falling into his eyes. When the man brushed his brown hair back, Brian took a picture of his face as he sat down in front of the computer, and began a facial recognition program to find out who this man might be.

Michael needed to check his email accounts and make sure things were ok at home. His parents still worried about him and his brother.....whew, his brother, always some news of a girl, a fight, a new job or something. One email was from Manuel, an old friend from undergraduate days. Manuel, from Columbia, was a biological researcher doing something with cloning, or some sort of DNA activity. Manuel and Michael could not talk well or at any length about what they each were doing, as the language of science and the humanities had too large a gulf to cross.

Manuel wrote that he was completing his dissertation on cloning extinct animals. Somehow, (and here Manuel wrote in very simple easy to understand language, so a Humanities major like Michael could understand), scientists were able to find the DNA material in ancient cellular materials, and through varied processes, extract enough of the necessary components to be able to clone the animal today. The team had already cloned an early amphibian and had recently "birthed" an early form of mammal. Manuel was excited to tell Michael that this research had been accepted, and scientific journals were calling him wanting the story. He was completing the final parts of his dissertation and hoped to complete it in just a few days.

Of course Michael was very happy for his friend, but also disappointed. While his friends were getting their doctorates and moving on to teaching and researching in prestigious universities, he was…was what? HE had found the original shroud of Jesus! THAT'S WHAT! So there, Manuel! You might be able to clone an extinct animal. He had Jesus. He had the cloth the body of Christ was wrapped in. He had the very cloth that had been wrapped around the dead, bloody, bruised body of Jesus. He *had* DNA!

The thought crashed into Michael's head like a truck. What if? No! It couldn't be possible. But, what if there was blood? Could? No, Michael could not go there.....yet. He would email Manuel and ask about this cloning, and how much blood or whatever was needed, and what condition it had to be in....but no. Somehow, even though Michael was not even close to being religious, his days in Sunday school when he was a boy kicked in, and he knew he was messing with the things of God, and did not want to go there.

The email was sent to Manuel. Brian read it, and again a long, low whistle escaped from between his teeth. Of course! This was how to bring Jesus *back to the earth*! If the tiny sample of DNA could be obtained from the dried blood on the shroud, then the scientists on Brian's payroll could clone this DNA and he, Brian, would be instrumental in bringing the return of the Lord Jesus Christ to the earth to judge all of the sinful men and women. Two phone calls had to be made quickly.

Michael and Sladjana were dressed and walking out the door. They had Michael's car, and they were going to the monastery. Sladjana had her laptop and was already connected, so the GPS could take them the shortest route to the monastery. As they drove along, Michael began to tell Sladjana about Manuel and his research on cloning extinct animals. Sladjana grew pale as she realized the possibilities of what could be done with the DNA from the blood on the shroud.

"So, dear lady," Michael squeezed her hand. "What do we do with the shroud after we find it? Do we keep it or turn it over to someone? Who do we trust with something like this?"

She deliberated his question for a moment before finally answering him, "Who *can* we trust with such power? This is power, and religion is power. Whoever has this can create a force against *world* powers."

"Yeah, but think of the good that could be done. Miracles, end of starvation, end of wars, end of petty people and the beginning of peace, love, grace. Could you imagine Jesus on CNN telling that Cooper guy a thing or two? Or maybe on FOX and finally getting the last word on O'Reilly? That would be classic! Then Jesus could be in the UN. He could solve world problems, end the fat cats getting fatter and skinning the little guys. Jesus would be the answer!"

"Would it really? Has religion ever solved any problem, Michael? Religion kills, starves, alienates, spreads hate, and judges. I do not want to be any part of that. "

"So, who do we give it to? " he asked again, knowing that she didn't have the answer either.

"I do not know" Sladjana pulled within herself and began typing randomly on her laptop, seemingly frustrated.

Brian had heard and seen all of this exchange. "So they know. They see the possibilities and they know. But they *don't* know what to do. Well, I can help them with that problem." A smile spread upon Brian's thin lips.

Brian had called Meredith and Warner just before the two had left her apartment. They had entered the place and began to look around. Warner soon found, among Sladjana's frilly underwear,(which he enjoyed touching, smelling and even putting one in his pocket), Branislav's letter she had copied a few days earlier. This was scanned and sent to Brian. This further evidence confirmed the next phone call Brian had to make. He called Brother Bob. After talking to Bob, Brian gave his two men the GPS coordinates of the monastery, and told them to get there and wait unseen for further instructions.

Michael and Sladjana drove between the broken buildings. Michael felt comfortable here. Sladjana had never been here before and was scared. She did not understand why she was overcome with such an unsettling feeling, but she felt darkness creeping at the edges. She looked around; and seeing no one did not help her unease.

Michael walked briskly around the debris, the broken stones, tree roots, and tilting walls, into the chapel. He bowed and crossed himself. He thought he had best act in a respectful manner since he was soon to be touching the blood of the Son of God. He stared at the front wall behind the altar as he walked up the aisle. There was nothing to see. A blank stone wall presented itself with no obvious markings. For the next hour Sladjana and Michael walked around the front of the chapel, touched all over the wall, looked from different angles, but could see nothing that might indicate any hiding place. Michael looked for the nail holes where the crucifix might have hung, but could not find even a trace of where they might have been.

Sladjana backed away, got on her laptop and began researching the religious practices of these monasteries. She didn't know what she was looking for, but they were not finding anything with the current approach.

Michael returned to the place where he first knelt at the altar, where he first saw the arrow. He bowed and found the arrow. "What would a holy man do?" he whispered to himself, shaking his head, with the frustration of knowing he was close. He bowed, looked up, and saw nothing.

Sladjana put her hands on her hips, giving a look of finally understanding, and then yelled at him, "They had no crucifix! It seems these monasteries had nothing on the front walls, unlike Roman Catholic monasteries that had a crucifix. So we know nothing is missing. But what do we do now?"

Michael was beyond frustrated and just did not know the answer. His knees hurt on the uneven stones. He decided to simply lie down where he was kneeling; if nothing else to take the pressure off of his knees. He laid down and saw the arrow just beneath his nose, and then he saw something. Looking at the front wall, close to the floor, under a ledge of stone, was a hole.

"Where a holy man would look? On his face prostrate before God. This is where a holy man would be!"

He finally understood. A feeling of overwhelming intensity washed over him, "I FOUND IT!"

Sladjana jumped and the laptop almost fell to the floor.

Brian jumped and spilled his coffee all over his blue shirt.

"I FOUND IT!" Michael began crawling to the opening. Sladjana could see nothing. Brian could see even less. But Michael saw the black hole. He touched the outside edge of the hole with his right hand, and felt the coolness and smoothness of the opening. He put his hand inside the hole. He reached in past his elbow, and almost had his entire arm in the hole, before he touched something. It felt like leather. A surge went through his body. He was touching that which had touched the body of Jesus! Michael paused. He prayed. For the first time in his adult life, he thanked God for His help.

Michael pulled the bag carefully out of the hole, and there it was. A leather bag very similar to the bag he had found under the altar. Sladjana had quickly joined him on the floor, and was now touching the bag. She caressed it lovingly and cautiously with the tips of her fingers.

Brian was listening. The laptop was askew, so he could not see anything, except the ceiling of the chapel. But he heard whispers and laughter. He heard relief and joy. Brian knew they had found the shroud. He called Meredith and his sidekick. He told them to stay close to the chapel, and to try to find out, without being seen, what was found. He also told them to begin making preliminary plans to ensure the shroud was in Texas within 24 hours.

Meredith and Warner moved to the doors and listened. They got inside the chapel without being seen and discovered that these two people were not even looking for them. They could have strolled up the aisle and sat on the front chairs. No one would have noticed. They also began consideration of how to get the bag to Texas.

Michael and Sladjana stared at the bag for long minutes. Each wanted to touch it, but somehow neither wanted to open it. Finally, Michael lifted the bag and opened the top. A glow began to illuminate the ceiling of the chapel. All in the chapel saw this uncanny shining coming from inside of the bag. It was a soft glow at first, becoming brighter, until eventually the light was almost blinding. Michael and Sladjana looked, first at each other, and then down into the bag. They placed their hands in the bag, and their fingers grazed the edge of the glowing cloth. Warner and Meredith looked at each other, and each knew that God was involved in this, big time.

Chapter 12

Brother Bob was in reverie. He sat in the back chairs of the sanctuary, listening to the choir practice for the upcoming Christmas season. That wonderful music was telling the story of the birth of Christ, and the coming of the Savior of the world. He sat and allowed the beauty and majesty of the story, ideas of his God's love, and Christ's mercy to wash over him.

Suddenly he felt a constriction in his chest, at first he thought it was a heart attack, but he came to an awareness that the voice of God was speaking to him. He almost felt as if God Himself was sitting next to him and whispering in his ear.

"Bob, you are my chosen vessel. I selected you among many others in this generation for a unique task. I have told you before that you will not die before you see the coming of My Son to the earth. It is time for Him to come. I will show my majesty in bringing people together. I will bring religion, music, the media, science, and the entire world together to show them My Son. I will show you the blood. You will take the blood and create the Kingdom of God. I will be bringing events to you in the next several days. You are to follow the way your heart goes, and this will bring about the return of the King of Kings."

Bob sat listening, pondering, and trying to put into words what God had just told him. He, Bob, little 'ole Bob from Podunk Texas, was chosen by the Almighty of the Universe in this day, in this time, to bring about the return of Christ! Yes! He had known all his life that he was indeed a chosen vessel. He had known that God had His hand upon his soul and life. Now was his time, now was the chosen generation, and *he* was the chosen leader. He swelled with pride and satisfaction.

And then questions began coming. What *was* going to happen? How *was* he to know what to do? How would the devil come to thwart these plans? How would he unite religion, science, and the entire world? And what did this mean about the blood? And how would he create God's Kingdom, wasn't this God's job?

As if on cue, Brother Bob's cell phone rang. He pulled it from his pocket and saw that it was Brian calling him. No one could hear him as they talked, so opening the phone, and with all this recent revelation from God upon his soul, he listened. Brian told Brother Bob that indeed he had been right about something happening in the world. He had discovered what was going on. They had to meet. Bob and Brian were to meet in Bob's office in one hour.

Brian took the data he had collected from Sladjana's computer, the photos, the documents, and all the other information he had gathered, and created a rather well produced power point presentation. This was the only way to get Bob's attention, and ensure that he understood what was going on. Brian loaded the presentation on a memory stick and walked to Brother Bob's office. Upon entering he walked to Bob's desk, loaded the data, and projected the power point onto the wall. He walked Bob through all sections of the discoveries, and how these two individuals had somehow stumbled upon the very shroud of Jesus while they were fornicating somewhere in Serbia. Indeed, Brian ended cleverly with a few slides on cloning, and the possibilities of taking the DNA from the blood on the shroud to clone a savior for the world. After all, this is what the world needed, the second coming of Christ.

At this suggestion, Bob turned to look directly into Brian's eyes. *Had* he heard what he *thought* he had heard? That the bloody stains from this shroud, the *bloody* stains...... could return Jesus to the earth, and thus the Kingdom of God would come? Was it possible to obtain this shroud and create a clone of Jesus?

Brother Bob shuddered and quickly sat down in the overstuffed chair. He grabbed for a cold glass of water, and held the glass to his forehead. God was moving here. God had come from eternity to dwell among them, in this office. God was working divine miracles, using modern technology, for His eternal purposes. God was here. Bob bowed his head and worshipped.

Bob's mind was awhirl with possibilities. What *could* and *would* happen for the world Christian community if Jesus were to return to the earth? Wicked men, ungodly governments, and non-religious people would be taken down. The liberal media would be shut down, as Jesus spoke and these unbelieving news people would fall on their knees on camera, and turn to the Lord. Power would return to the church, and God would use men, like Brother Bob, to stand with the Lord as the new Apostles. Oh the glory of

God *would* come, and all wickedness around the world would cease.

When Bob looked up again, he placed his eyes upon Brian, and simply stated, "I want that shroud."

Brian looked back. "You will have it by the end of the week, I am sure."

With that Brian walked out of the room. Bob continued to sit, and simply stare out his office window into the skyline of Houston. Jesus was coming back to earth. He, Brother Bob, would bring it to pass. The morning passed, with Bob simply staring out the window.

Brian walked back to his office with a complete plan forming in his mind. He had the men in place. He would get the shroud, and have it flown to his office. In the meantime, he would get some of the other researchers to begin finding out everything they could in regard to the cloning process. Then, he would have to find a genetic physicist who could be coerced, however necessary, to carry out this act of God. Christ was coming again, and Brian Sharp would make damn certain of it.

Brian phoned Warner, and told him to obtain the shroud. "I do not care what happens to the two people, but make sure it's an accident, and no one can talk afterwards. I want that package in Texas 24 hours from now. Do what we pay you for my brother."

With that order, Brian knew that within 24 hours the package would be in his hands. He would move now to make necessary plans. He would allow these other men to do whatever they needed. And he would go, and prepare a place for the most important discovery in two thousand years.

Warner and Meredith withdrew from the chapel, and into a copse of trees. They talked for a while and planned what to do. Meredith went to Michael's car, and cut the brake line so that some of the fluid would leak, but the brakes would work for awhile. Warner returned to the chapel, to keep an eye on these two. When they started to gather their stuff, and looked as if they were leaving, Warner met Meredith at their own car, and they waited.

Michael and Sladjana were full of joy, but kept the excitement to a minimum, at least as far as anyone would have noticed. They did not know what to do yet, but they were going to return to her apartment, and then decide. They each got in the car, and Michael began driving away. As he went down a hill, he applied the brakes and found the pedal went to the floor. He began pumping the brakes and trying to slow down.

Michael looked at Sladjana, with deep rooted fear in his eyes. He knew something was wrong, on many levels. Having no brakes was too much of a coincidence at this particular point in his life. He knew immediately someone was after them, and he knew it was about the Shroud.

Sladjana saw the fear in his eyes, and grabbed the leather bag, hugging it to her chest. As she looked up to see what was happening, a tree was looming closer. Michael could not stop or even slow down. The road was full of curves, and even though Michael tried to control the car, they hit the tree hard, and Sladjana's world went black. Michael's thought just after he hit the tree, and just before he lost consciousness, was "Great, the one time I thank God, someone tries to kill me."

Warner and Meredith following close behind, pulled up behind the wrecked car and got out. No one was around; this certainly was a desolate road. They each moved to a door, and felt the neck of the person in the seat. Neither felt a pulse. Meredith removed the leather bag, now a little bloody, from the grip of Sladjana's lifeless body, and walked back to the car. There, Warner was already inside, ready to drive away. Without a word, Meredith began wiping the fresh blood off the bag, while they drove toward the airport. A call was made, and a private jet would be waiting for them on the tarmac. It would provide them safe passage to Texas. God was with them, all the way.

Chapter 13

The plane was cruising at 32,000 feet. Meredith and Warner, being the good soldiers they were, had fallen asleep. They had accomplished their task; they had the full leather bag. Not knowing what was next, they slept. Texas would arrive soon enough.

Dr. Doreen Sage, visiting ER physician, was working over the two bodies that had been found on a deserted roadside. Somehow, they had been found on a rough road, out there somewhere away from civilization. Since she had arrived here from Toronto six months ago, she had seen this sort of thing happen several times already. Someone would find a wreck, and bring the wounded in. Many times they were DOA. These two were, almost, but not quite. She worked, giving orders to nurses, cutting off bloody clothing, and wondering what had kept this man and woman alive. She worked quickly, and with much precision. If their lives could be saved, she would do everything in her power to make sure they would be.

Brian Sharp was reading over all the literature his teams had assembled about cloning. The subject matter became increasingly fascinating to him, as he submersed himself in various articles, absorbing as much information as possible.

Brother Bob had locked himself away in his office. He knew his life was about to change. He needed to pause, pray, plan, and then make some moves. He was awaiting a report from Sharp, but until then, he needed to prepare. So somehow, they were going to extract some DNA from the blood on the Shroud, they were going to do something with it, and it was going to grow into a human being. But that would take 20 or 30 years! He could not wait that long. Surely there was a way to grow this child at a more accelerated pace.

But where would they grow it? There were laws here in America, and too many in the religious community would frown, and even condemn him, if they knew what he was doing. No, it had to be out of America, and in a place where no one would know. Then, after the birth an announcement would be made, and no one would ever have to know about the cloning. It would be a miraculous birth. He would personally officiate and control all contacts and reports. He was going to bring Jesus back to earth. He was going to control, under God's control of course, the Kingdom of God on earth. Finally, there would be a way to end sin, homosexuality, and abortion; a way to end greed and corruption, wars and disease. Finally the church would arise with power and freedom, so the world would know Almighty God, Jehovah, was the *only* God. Those Muslims and their Allah, those Buddhists, and any of those other heathen people, would bow to their knees at the King of Kings and Lord of Lords. Brother Bob would be there to see it all, so he needed answers.

He had to establish control as the head of this operation. He began to write an email to Brian Sharp, in order to begin the process of creating the team, and laying the groundwork for the plans.

"This baby has to be born in Israel. The ministry already owns a rather large kibbutz in northern Israel. We will adapt places there, and bring in people to birth the baby and take care of him.

I know you, Brian, and I know you have connections with professionals who can do the cloning. We must keep all aspects compartmentalized, so no group really knows what the other groups are doing. We must maintain secrecy, and ensure that no one knows what we are doing. One day we will present Him to the world and then all will be out. But for now, this is top secret.

We must speed the process of the child's growth. I heard of a recent Nobel Prize winner, whose research determined the aging process of chromosomes. I am attaching a link to the article regarding his work. And thus perhaps we can find a way to speed up the chromosomes, so cloning and growth can happen quicker. I need you to research this with some calls.

We need a Media consultant to begin, even now, preparing the groundwork to keep what we are doing secret, which will provide a smokescreen to any who might look into this, and to prepare for future announcements. Some lucky journalist will have the story of the century, so it should not be too difficult to find someone we can trust.

I also need a family. I need a mother to birth this baby. I need a family to raise this child. I need a community. I will use the kibbutz setting. I need a woman, a virgin; someone even named Mary would be appropriate, but I am realistic, so her name is not of consequence.

I need a team I can trust: people with no questions as to loyalty, commitment to God, and to myself. This is a huge event, and the world will now change.

So, Brian, create a team. We need to move on this.

I will make sure you personally are very well compensated, and I am giving you anything you and your team need to complete this task."

Brother Bob sent the email and felt relieved. The plan was evolving. Bob had learned through the years to give people a job, and then allow them to work. This was a big task, but he would take care of Brian and his team.

Brian looked at the email and read it again, making sure he understood every detail. Indeed a new and trusted team, actually *teams*, would be needed. He had plenty of money personally, but more money was always a good thing. Things were going to move now and in the next few years, so Brian wanted to ensure he was well compensated for what lay ahead. More and different plans were beginning to form in his mind's eye.

Brian would ensure that Brother Bob would get his child. But what was really needed to combat sin in this world and to create the Kingdom of God, was to destroy those who live in sin embracing lifestyles that spit in the face of God. What was needed was an army of soldiers that had been cloned from the blood of Christ. Such an army would rise up and lead the world to God and His ways. Brian could make sure such an army arose, and he would even help lead it.

Brian formed the necessary teams. He had men and women scattered across the world. The next few days were a blur of pulsating activity. The Shroud was taken from Warner and Meredith, and given to a top notch team at Baylor University. They extracted the human tissues, and then the DNA from the linen fabric.

Brian had already contacted the experts in cloning at the University of Hamburg in Germany. They were to grow the cells, and create a living organism that could be inserted into a womb. The university would be very well compensated, and no questions were to be asked.

He next found a likely candidate to give birth to the child. She was a perfect human specimen, and she was even named Mary. She was Brother Bob's niece, the daughter of his wayward brother Allen. Surely God had prepared such a vessel, as this Mary, to carry His son. Even the name was proof that God was involved in this situation. Mary had come to Bob several years ago, wanting to get away from her father, and his sinful lifestyle. Bob had raised Mary as his own daughter. She was now 17 years old, and a virgin. She promised her uncle to be abstinent, and had even gone through the "promise" course at the church. She was drug and disease free. Mary had never even been kissed by a boy. She was open to her uncle's idea after Brother Bob explained things, of course not everything, to her.

Mary was flown to Germany, and impregnated with the growing group of cells. They had already multiplied to 16 cells when they were surgically attached to her uterine wall. After a few days of observation, Mary flew on to the Kibbutz in northern Israel, where she was to live the next months until the birth.

While Brian was busy accomplishing this amazing feat, he had made some phone calls to Henry, the leader of Omega. Henry was an intense man, who desired God's Kingdom upon the earth in his lifetime. He was willing to do almost anything to make this happen.

Brian met with Henry in North Carolina, after he diverted one of his trips to Germany, to fly into Raleigh. He had rented a car and driven to a little town called Washington on the Tar River. There, he boarded Henry's private yacht docked at the city waterfront. As the boat coasted down the Pamlico Sound, Brian told Henry the complete plan of Brother Bob to clone Jesus; and to raise him as the Messiah of the world, to spread Christianity, and to topple nations.

To say the least, Henry was intrigued. He immediately saw all possibilities. He could raise an army of divine men who would gather all heathens, destroy all non-Christian nations, and set up the kingdom of God on earth. He could trust these men to do right, after all they would be cloned from Christ himself, and to reign supreme. He would lead such men to rule the world. Brian and Henry agreed to monetary terms. Brian walked away 15 million dollars richer; and Henry kept, on his boat, the dish of viable and growing cells from the shroud of Jesus.

Henry returned to his camp further down the river, and began the process of building such an army.

Brian flew on to Houston to invest his money, build the Kingdom, and follow the route God had chosen for him.

The ministry of Brother Bob continued to grow. Bob expanded his empire to include most evangelical churches and groupings. With the money that flowed in from widows, families, businesses, and governments; his media empire bought CNN and FOX news. He controlled the daily diet of American news. He did not change much immediately, but his firm hand of control began a process of change, only slightly noticeable to the astute observer, and in his opinion there were few astute observers of these broadcasts.

Dr. Sage worked on Michael and Sladjana for more hours than her time allowed, but she felt deep within herself that she had to take care of them. Nothing she knew medically would help them. They were slipping away and there was nothing she could do.

Michael felt a deep and frightening darkness creep into his soul. He didn't know what had brought him into this darkness, but he was definitely engulfed by it. However, there was a light on the edge of his fingers. This light was spreading up his arms and into his chest. A sharp pain surged through him and he took a deep and gasping breath. He was awake.

Suddenly the ground shook, as a minor earthquake shook Serbia, and varied cities around the region.

Dr. Sage stepped back, startled, the shaking ground caused her to lose her footing. Then the man lunged upward, and air caught in his throat. Something was happening that she did not understand and could not explain by medicine, but the bleeding had stopped, and the wounds on his head seemed to be healing on their own. She looked to the woman, and suddenly she too bent forward, and breathed deeply. Something or someone had brought these two back to life, and was healing them in a seemingly divine manner. As she stared dumbfounded at the two patients, wounds healed and machines began beeping normal readings. She looked at the time; it was 2:57 am.

Michael looked around and saw Sladjana lying on the next table. She looked at him and their eyes locked. They both knew that a miracle had happened in their lives. All Michael could recall was sitting in the car, then the sudden crash as the tree came through the windshield, and then the blackness. But he was dying, there was no other answer. What had happened? He looked at his hand, that hand where the light shone from his fingers. There was dried blood…not his blood. Could it be that some of the blood from the shroud had touched his fingers? Could that divine blood from Jesus save him, even after two thousand years?

Michael was ready to walk out of the hospital. He stood from his bed, and began removing wires and monitoring devices. There was nothing wrong with him now. He was sure that the same blood had saved Sladjana, and that she also was ready to leave. Dr. Sage did not know what to do. Surely these two needed to be held for observation, but she did not know what to observe. So she released them.

After they walked out the door, Dr. Sage called the number she had been meaning to call since the almost dead couple was brought in. Not finding any other number in the pockets of either of them, the only number was one of Fadia, a reporter for Aljazeera News. Dr. Sage called her and told her about her friend. Fadia thanked her.

Fadia Merenni immediately began researching on the web about her friend, this Michael guy, and any reports of accidents. She called the local police and discovered that, indeed, they had hit a tree and were taken almost dead to the local hospital. She next called Sladjana and talked with concern to her friend. While talking, Sladjana, in her frustration and need to vent, told the whole story to Fadia. Ms. Merenni listened, took notes, and learned all about the monastery, leather bag, shroud, and accident.

A story was on the Aljazeera News website within two hours.

A dilapidated monastery, a leather bag, and some deep university research have allowed an academic couple from Serbia to find new discoveries and truth about the

Shroud of Turin. The Turin Shroud has traditionally been viewed as the burial cloth of the Christian Jesus. This shroud was supposedly used to wrap his dead body after he was crucified. Tradition holds that the cloth moved from Jerusalem to Constantinople (now Istanbul), and then during the invading wars from Europe known as the Crusades, the cloth was stolen and taken to the Vatican in Rome.

But the couple, who have requested their identities remain anonymous, have discovered what could be the real shroud.

In later editions of this story I will show their research, the diaries they have found, and the manner in which someone has supposedly tried to kill them to destroy the evidence of the shroud.

Fadia looked over her short story and was pleased. She hoped she was not taking too much advantage of her friendship with Sladjana, but this was an important story, and needed to be out there. She was going to try to get the research and all the other information she could from her friend, so the story could be expanded, and thus her career would possibly grow as well.

The story was now out. Of course it got buried with all the earthquakes that had occurred that night, but the story was read by many around the world.

The computer room in Houston picked up on the further story. Brian was notified, and he was somewhat miffed that his two special experts had not completed their task. In the briefing upon their return they had both stated the two researchers were dead. Somehow a major mistake had been made, and Brian would have to take care of it in the days ahead.

Michael and Sladjana sat at a café just around the corner from the hospital. Each was quiet and said nothing. Finally, after staring for too long into their half-filled glasses, they looked up and into each other's eyes. They had been through too much for any two people the past few days. Now they had faced death and miracles together. They talked about the final moments they recalled. There were no clues to what happened to them, or who was behind it. Someone had caused their car to crash. Someone had thought they were dead. Someone had stolen the shroud. What now?

Whoever had stolen the shroud was willing to murder for it. Why would they want it? What could they do about it all? If the people who had the shroud could kill them once, then they could be killed again.

Chapter 14

The rumbling began in the east part of the city. Earthquakes were not a concern in Rome, but this rumbling seemed to be moving across the city toward the Vatican itself. When it finally reached the Cathedral of St. Peter, it stopped moving. The rumbling seemed to stay put and just move the earth up and down for what seemed like minutes.

The government office that monitored earthquakes later stated that it lasted only two and half minute's total. But to those in bed in the varied dormitories and suites scattered throughout the Holy See, it seemed like many, many minutes.

Pope Francis Paul awoke with a start when the rumbling was finally felt. He had been Pope only 3 months. His predecessor had died suddenly, and this former priest from Guatemala was still overwhelmed with all the Cardinals, and powers the Vatican had to hide. It was 2:57 am. He had gone to bed only an hour ago. He had barely had time to close his eyes and now he was awake.

Deep in his heart, as he lay in bed and allowed the rumbling of the quaking earth to settle out of his soul, this simple, holy man felt a pressure. He knew it was not a heart attack; it was more a spiritual pressure, as if the voice of God was trying to break through the accoutrements and vestments of the Office, and trying to talk to the simple priest as He had so many years ago.

Finally Samuel (for that was the name his mother had given him, and that was still the name he called himself) got out of bed, put on a thick robe, and walked out on the balcony of his room. He did not turn on a light, for then someone would come in and try to help him. He wanted to be left alone, and listen quietly.

He looked in the direction of St. Peter's Cathedral. He knew there were many basements under the church, and inside those basements were too many treasures the church had collected through the centuries. As he looked, he felt in his spirit that something was happening in the realm of eternity. Something was breaking through, and God seemed to be trying to tell him something.

Samuel paused, and from his heart told the Lord that he was listening, and would wait for the clarity to come. Samuel waited.

Deep within those basements a security guard was walking through the corridors on his nightly rounds. When the earthquake rumbled, he was in the deepest of the treasuries and felt the ground shaking, moving up and down, and acting more like a wave beneath his feet. The movement of the earth seemed to be centering and concentrating on one particular vault with a large wooden door. He looked through the window in the door, and saw a glow in the far corner of the room. A large box, about the size of a coffin, had a glow coming from the inside, as the wave was concentrating all of its energies right on that box.

The guard could not believe what he was seeing and knew he would never tell anyone. What he did know was that something or someone was putting a lot of focus on that room, on that box. Nothing else in the room had any type of light, only that big, heavy looking box. He did not know what was in the box, and did not care. He was scared. He quickly walked out of the depths, and continued his rounds in the upper levels. He had read too many science fiction and horror books to want to stay around and see some type of alien.

But the glow continued, and the object in the box received the energy and power from the forces of the universe. After 3000 years of no use, the box emanated with the power of God again.

Samuel was almost falling asleep; when deep within his heart he knew God was speaking.

"Samuel, I have placed you here for such a time as this. It is time for my Son to return to earth and reign again. You have shown your heart to be after godliness, and now all your sacrifices and struggles will be rewarded"

Samuel quickly revived and slipped from his chair to fall to his knees.

"This earthquake is MY power showing various earthly peoples I am in control, and I am doing MY thing. Many will try to control the next few years for their own prestige and power. Do not be fooled. All you will see will not be from me. You will know what is from me, and what is not from me. Walk carefully, and prepare your people."

Samuel found himself on the floor prostrate before God. He stayed there the remainder of the night. He did not sleep. He meditated on these Holy words. What was he to do? What could and should he do? How to prepare his people around the world? How not to be fooled? Why so cryptic? Why didn't God simply state what was needed?

When morning came, Samuel was dressed and ready for the day. He had no answers, but he knew a direction to proceed. He would have a two pronged approach. After breakfast and morning prayers, he called his most trusted friend and advisor, Father Jerome. Jerome had been a childhood friend. They had gone through seminary together, and Samuel had brought him to Rome for the friendship, the closeness he needed, and for someone to advise him without the politics and schemes of the Cardinals.

He told Jerome what had happened in the night. He told his friend the words of God and the questions that had come to mind. He and Jerome talked all these things over throughout the morning. Several important meetings had to be canceled. Various administrators in the Vatican grew impatient and frustrated with this new pope, but the private meeting with the two friends would not be interrupted.

Samuel asked his friend to find answers. He did not know what answers might come, but this late night visitation was very important and dealing with the return of the Lord Jesus. The Pope took to heart the admonition not to be fooled by what was going to happen.

Jerome left and returned to his office. Jerome had contacts all over the world. He simply opened his laptop and began writing emails to friends and colleagues. Time would bring information.

The second meeting Pope Francis Paul had was with the central meeting of the Cardinals. These few men had the power of the Vatican. They kept the traditions and treasures of the Church.

The Pope began the meeting by asking how the church was situated for the return of Christ to the earth. He looked around and saw that these men had not considered this prospect of life. They had spent years keeping the church intact, profitable, and growing. To begin the process of actually planning on the supposed return of the Lord Jesus cut into their plans and long term goals.

Pope Francis Paul asked these men to create committees, and form working groups, to begin to plan what the church should do to prepare for the soon return of the Lord. To plan how they could ensure they were not being fooled by schemes and subterfuge, and how they could know in truth that the Lord had returned.

The men agreed to form some groups of priests to look into these questions. The meeting adjourned with a prayer.

Samuel knew these men of the red capes and hats believed he was some yokel from the mountains. He was not even a member of the College of Cardinals before he was elected Pope. He was indeed a simple priest from the mountains. But he knew God's voice. He knew God's word in this world today. He knew God's people.

He had begun the process of his two pronged approach. He knew Jerome would try his best to discover what was needed. He had no faith in the working groups of priests, but he gave them the benefit of the doubt, and prayed God might intervene in these groups, so His will would be done.

Samuel told his assistants not to bother him for the remainder of the day. He locked himself in his rooms and simply meditated. Eternity was coming to touch the earth. Jesus, his blessed Lord, was soon to come back and claim His own. Samuel, simple priest, was allowed to be Pope, the Father to the people of the Church at such a time. He wanted to tread very lightly. His days were full of much wasted scheduled time, but in between times, Pope Francis Paul walked carefully, and thought on these things, as he held them close to his heart.

Chapter 15

From the south the rumbling of the earthquake moved up the edge of the Carpathian Mountains and the Black Sea. The wave of movement went quickly through Kiev, and at 4:57 was swelling into Red Square, to stop at the onion domed cathedral, *Cathedral of St. Vasily the Blessed*, or as most know it, St. Basil's Cathedral. Built in 1555, and dominating central Moscow, this church houses the artifacts of the Old Roman Empire.

It seems by the time Rome fell in 476 AD, most of the important documents, treasures, and artifacts had already been moved to Constantinople for safe keeping. As the Vandals took Rome, the Roman Empire settled into controlling what remained from the city, in what is now Turkey.

When Constantinople fell in 1453, these important treasures had followed the Orthodox Church leadership to their new headquarters in Moscow. Thus, Moscow and the Orthodox Church see themselves as the true historical link not only to the Roman Empire, but to the true roots and practices of Christianity. The Patriarch of Moscow sees himself as the true head of the church worldwide.

The rumbling moved to the sub-basements of the cathedral. Deep within, in a room similar to a crypt, where past Patriarchs were entombed and treasures from ages past were stored, a small box began to glow. The movement of the earth seemed to stop and concentrate on this box. It was a wooden box, not even a meter square. The box had been forgotten hundreds of years before, and no one alive knew of its existence or specialness in the realms of eternity, but it glowed with supernatural warmth and light.

No one saw this spectacle. No one witnessed eternity coming to Red Square and the *Cathedral of St. Vasily the Blessed*. No one heard anything.

Men and women around the large city were beginning to wake and consider this new day. Some couples turned to each other and made love. Some turned away and returned to sleep. A few men and women felt a deep rumbling in their souls, but could not place the feeling. Some children opened their eyes, looked into the darkness, and whispered a simple prayer to God.

The spirit of the Most High lingered over the city, but could find no one who would or could listen to His voice, His message. No one knew that God had come and was coming again very soon.

The box glowed. The rumbling stopped. God had come and no one knew.

Chapter 16

Traffic in Tehran was already beginning to get busy when the rumbling wave of the earth's movement came through the city at 5:27 am. Several accidents ensued, and many cars simply pulled over and stopped, until the wave of movement passed. Earthquakes were common, and no one really paid too much attention to them.

The wave came from the west, and moved under the Black Sea, bypassing the Caspian Sea and into the city from the West. The rumbling came to the huge complex of the Azadi Tower in the center of the city. The wave stopped when it came to the actual tower, and to the basement of the museum that houses the artifacts and treasures of the Persian Empire. These days it also housed the treasures of the Babylonian Empire. Treasures that were looted from the museums in Baghdad, Iraq, when the city fell to American invaders, were now here. These treasures were taken to keep the history of this area safe from Zionist foreigners.

In this museum was an artifact, taken originally from the Temple in Jerusalem, when the Romans destroyed the city in 93 AD. The soldiers, who took this city, its treasures and its people in that year, destroyed the city and culture of Israel. In these treasures was a holy artifact that eventually was sold by some soldiers to a group of merchants. These merchants took it home to Baghdad, and sold it to the royal treasury. It remained there for almost 2000 years (although a replica was given as a gift to the Patriarch in Constantinople); hidden deep, forgotten, behind boxes.

In 2004, Iranian Muslim clerics identified many items to be taken and made safe from the fallen city of Bagdad. This artifact was on the list. Now it resided deep within the Tower of Azadi. The rumbling centered on this corner of the museum, and the box hidden behind other boxes began to glow, and emanate light. No one noticed, but the glow was powerful and bright.

A simple shopkeeper, Abdullah, who sold oranges and lemons from his cart along the road, was in prayer at the time of the earthquake. He had parked his cart and stepped aside into an alley, because a burden of prayer and of seeking God had come strongly upon him.

As he knelt in prayer and in quietness, he seemed to hear the voice of God speaking to his very soul.

"I am pleased that you seek me, Abdullah. I know you and care so very much for you. Of all the men today, I am more pleased with you and your simple heart. I am sending Isa Masih (Jesus Messiah) to return to the earth to gather His people and judge the wicked. Many will be fooled in the coming years, but I want you to seek Me, and I will lead you and your family to truth. Walk carefully my child."

Abdullah lay prostrate in the alley. He could not move. He heard the traffic increasing in the roadway, but he was overwhelmed with the words from God. He did not know what to do, so he lay there and meditated upon these words.

At that same time the lead cleric of the Iranian people, Grand Ayatollah Ali Sistani, was in his daily prayers and meditation. He felt the earth move but thought nothing of it. He had felt the earth move many times in his life, and knew this was not how God worked. God worked in His word, the Holy Koran, and through his clerics. He continued his daily readings and prayers.

Later in the morning, when the routine was in full swing, a secretary came in to his office with a print out of a small article from Aljazeera. It was Fadia Merenni's article about the search for the Shroud. The secretary had thought it important to disturb the Ayatollah with this perhaps important news.

Upon reading the article, Sistani became quite concerned. He told his secretary to call a meeting of the leading clerics for later that afternoon. Then Sistani paced around his office considering the implications of this article. Of course, there was no truth to the shroud, for the Prophet Jesus did not rise from the dead, in fact according to his holy book, the prophet did not even die.

But, if the American Zionists believed the shroud to be true, if the people of the West believed this falsehood, then it would give them more power against the onward movement and enlargement of Islam around the world.

Sistani sat in the meeting and had his secretary read the article. The Ayatollah stood. As he looked around the room, at the men who controlled the religious aspects of Iran, and also sought to be the leaders of Islam around the world, he was pleased that such men as these would help make the necessary decisions.

"These words disturb me. We each know there is no truth in these words, but that will not stop the Zionists and the American Christians from using these words to advance their cause. If they somehow produce evidence of the resurrection, or even the provenance of the shroud, then our cause will be hurt and set back.

I want advice from you as to what we should do and how we should move forward."

Questions were asked and answered to the best of the leader's ability. He was finding they knew much less than they needed to know. Finally after three hours of fruitless discussion and questions, he asked that a committee be formed to seek the truth of what the Americans were doing. This group would travel, learn, write a report, and present their findings to the committee in 4 months.

The leaders agreed. A committee of five lower level clerics was formed. These men, each internet savvy and three having already visited the West, were ready to discover the truth.

Abdullah returned home after selling his produce and told his wife what had happened. She knew in her heart this was the word of God. They rejoiced together, but quietly. No one else in the family knew they were seeking God in such a way. They were overjoyed with praise to God as the day grew into evening, and the moon rose.

There was no rumbling anywhere else in the world. Only in these four specific areas: Belgrade, Rome, Moscow, and Tehran. The USGS (United States Geological Survey) had never seen an earthquake snake in such a fashion at the exact same minute over 10,000 miles and along no specific fault line, but there seemed to be little damage. Nothing significant had occurred. This earthquake was filed away as inconsequential. Many other important matters covered everybody's desks.

Chapter 17

Sladjana could not believe the past few weeks. She had found this man, found the shroud, been the victim of an attempted murder, experienced a miracle, did not know who to trust, and yet was falling in love and absolute wonder at this American who had stepped into her life. And then about two months after the accident, she knew she was pregnant. The problem was that they had not had sex since before the accident. Michael's medication prevented him from becoming erect, and she still felt too traumatized to go beyond hugging and kissing. Yet, she had missed two periods and she had all the symptoms explained on those websites.

She bought a pregnancy kit and indeed, it was positive. She was pregnant. How could she tell Michael? Would he believe she had been only with him?

Yet it was true. If it had not been Michael, and she knew she had not been with anyone else since they had met those months ago, what had happened?

The glowing light! It had healed her. It was still inside her. Could it have impregnated her? Was she with child as from God? This thing alive in her womb was the light from God; she was pregnant by miracle! Sladjana cried.

Michael was credulous. How could this happen? Immaculate, yeah right! When had she seen the other guy? Why had she seen the other guy? How *was* this guy? He found himself feeling angry and lost. He went for days without sleeping or eating.

Then one night Michael had a dream. It was Brother Branislav again. This was the third time this monk had come to him and led him to the truth. *Branislav invited Michael to walk with him along a stream. As they walked, a peace pervaded Michael. The monk turned to Michael and told him with a firmness of all eternity, "Believe. All things were possible to those who believed. The child was indeed to be born. Sladjana was indeed with child from the glow that came from the bag. The blood had not only restored their health but had now created a baby. Believe, Michael. But darkness does come. The glow, the blood, has been stolen by others. Others would grow the glow into a dark army. Others would try to use the blood of Jesus for their purposes and only darkness, only destruction, only evil would come. Michael, keep your baby as the way, teach him the truth, show him how to live."*

And then the monk was gone. Michael stood beside the peaceful stream in his dream and knew that he must keep his baby safe. He also knew he must rise and fight against whomever stole the shroud and cloned other babies. He must seek them out and destroy them.

Michael awoke covered in sweat. Sladjana lay peacefully and restfully on the pillow next to him. He stared at her. He looked at her swelling belly and felt a love, a peace, a belief, and knowledge. All was going to be ok. God was somehow involved in all of this. Sladjana was with child, not his, but not anyone else's either, it seemed.

It was of God. He looked with a growing love for her and the baby. He would do anything and everything possible to keep her and the baby safe. This child would grow in all things, and one day stand for God and the right things, against whatever darkness was out there looming.

Michael and Sladjana could not part. Michael stayed with Sladjana; building a life for her and the baby. He used the time to obtain a grant to research further into the Fourth Crusade, write a book on the subject, and slowly build a loving and trusting relationship with this woman, who had invited him in for coffee all those months ago.

They spent their spare time trying to rebuild the evidence they had lost. They had lost both leather bags and the copy of the letter Sladjana had made, but they had their memories. They recreated their research; but carefully this time. They wrote everything on paper and only went to an internet café to get online. Michael felt a deep urging from God, it seemed, to move forward with his research. He also did not want to allow those who had tried to kill him to know that he was still alive. He also felt a deep sense of vengeance. How dare anyone, any person try to kill him? How dare murder be on someone's mind? He would find these people, and he would wreak his vengeance on them. They had touched him, and he was very tired of being touched by people. Also, they had touched this woman that he had fallen in love with. How dare they touch her!

The months had flown by. Mary was only 60 days away from delivery. The media team hired for the PR was gearing up in two ways: presenting the world as a very bad place needing a savior, and showing how the leaders of various religions could lead in this modern world. Of course, the leaders of all religions were found wanting, except Christ. A team was in place, with no one knowing all the truth except Bob and Brian, to grow this child in all things good and right. Brother Bob continued to expound weekly from the pulpit in his church, and daily on his ever expanding worldwide TV and radio shows, about the coming return of Jesus, and how the world would change when God reigned again.

"Can you possibly imagine what the world will be like when He returns?

No more wars, no more politicians taking from the people to enrich themselves. No more armies needed to invade nations and kill innocents. No more waste of defense budgets and allowing children to die.

No more pain: He will heal. Where medical science ends, the Christ will touch and heal. No more waste of socialized medicines with the touch of Jesus.

No more tears: the godly will live and be blessed. Those who choose to follow Jesus will not be hurt by acts of nature, economic downturns, medical problems, and uncertainty of life.

No more fears: Jesus Himself will be among us. He will come to us and be like us. We need not fear colors of skin, economic backgrounds, and fear for our children or senior citizens. He will be near and will take care of us.

When Jesus returns, he will speak. He will bring nations together and cause them to lay down their arms and live peaceably together. If they will not, he will destroy them. He will bring an end to those who steal money and say it is good business. He will end all forms of sin and destruction and men and women and children will be in harmony.

When Jesus comes, He will stand in this pulpit and speak peace to you. We will stand and then bow before Him. Are you ready? Is there anything in your life He would not be happy with? Come to Him today and be ready."

Chapter 18

Henry felt like a king. He now had an army, albeit not yet born, but a powerful army nonetheless. As he looked over the glassed room and saw the thousands of dishes full of growing cells, he whispered his thanks to God for the blessings of knowledge, and he looked into the future and saw a mighty force destroying all that stood against the ways and manners of God. He saw himself as king; Henry had tears coursing down his cheeks.

As he stood in his headquarters in North Carolina, with a hurricane growing in destructive force of epic proportions outside, he was content that he had spared no expense in the construction of this laboratory. Nothing would destroy what he was meant to accomplish. Let the wind blow, let the heathen yell, let the forces of hell try to come near. He and this work were protected by a more sophisticated military force than even the American government had at its disposal. Nothing would touch him and his.

Soon the cells would grow and form the divine humans they were meant to be. He had his generals developing new military plans now for how to best use this army. He had his team leaders rewriting the training books, so these men would be soldiers to honor God and country.

In five years this army would be grown, trained, and ready to surge forth to finally destroy the forces of Islam, and take over the oil reserves of the Middle East. They would finally establish God's people, the Jews, as the sole owners of their homeland, given to Abraham centuries ago. Then they would surge forth to destroy homosexuals, liberal churches, and any others who stood in the way of God working His kingdom on this earth. Henry would fulfill the call of God on his life to make sure the earth submitted to God's ways.

Father Jerome had spent many hours and days learning, or at least trying to learn what might be happening around the world that his friend, Samuel (it was still not easy thinking of his best friend as being the Pope) was so concerned about.

Jerome had learned that a major Protestant ministry in Houston had declared the imminent return of Jesus, and seemed to be spending much money in Israel, and also on public relations to document this event. Strange, for many pastors had made such declarations in the past, but none had gone this far and stuck their neck out so much as to actually declare the soon and definite return of the Lord Jesus.

He gave his full report (appendix 1) to his friend the Pope. Then he went into a meditative retreat in northern Italy for the next six months. Jerome had to be quiet and simply contemplate God and the days ahead.

The Supreme council of the Ayatollahs met in a special conference room and Mohammed Faisal stood before them. He was very nervous; most of the clerics took this as simply being nervous standing in front of them.

Mohammed began by stating the other members of his team were ill from the change in food and water, and asked to kindly be excused. He was not feeling well, but did not want to keep the council waiting for his report.

Bound papers of the report were handed to each member. As they perused the charts, diagrams, and paragraphs, Mohammed began:

"We took many months so we could be sure of the conclusion. Basically, after exhaustive research, conversations with the leaders of churches, talking with members of these western Christian churches, and reading all the publications from many sources in America and Europe, we have determined that there is no plan at this time that is conclusive for the return of Jesus.

We could discover no proof of anything that might be in any way truthful about this falsehood regarding Isa. There are some false prophets who believe God is talking to them. They have a lot of money and some influence, but there is nothing beyond their insane notions of their simple beliefs.

There is nothing for us in Islam to be concerned about. The team has come to this firm and complete conclusion." [Please see his full and more complete report in Appendix 2]

With that, Mohammed Faisal turned and walked out of the room. The council turned to each other and with a quiet agreement moved to the next item on the agenda.

Michael Reagan was now the chair of the History department at Belgrade University. He had made so many connections through Sladjana and his research on the Shroud, as well as the Fourth Crusade, that when he earned his PhD, he decided to spurn that "Dr What's-her-name" in New Mexico, and stay here. He and Sladjana were happy. They had been living together for, well, they had never parted. The baby was ready to be born and both mother and child were healthy.

He was happy. His career was what he dreamed of those many months ago, back when he walked out of his cubicle in New Mexico. He was with the woman he had always dreamt about; she was more special, more loving than he could have ever hoped. He was almost a father. Although he was scared at first, as the months went by, he thought of the baby as his own, and grew more accustomed to the idea of fatherhood. He was a lucky man. They went out, had plenty of money and all was good. Still, sometimes there was a nagging dread in his heart each day. Why was he not content to live, but always drawn back to the leather bags, the crash, and the theft of the shroud? What more could he do now? He did not know, at least, not yet.

Sladjana was more than happy. A special man shared her bed and her life. She felt connected with him in life and death. The months had gone by and their time was perfect. She wanted nothing to change. They often talked of those heady days of rushing around trying to find the shroud. They spoke carefully of the death and life experience they each shared. They both wanted to know what had happened to the shroud, but she wanted to grow a life in her beloved city, with this man whom she loved more than her life.

She was ready to be a mother. She knew this child was of and from God; not able to quite understand everything about the conception; but at peace with it all. She was very pleased Michael was happy about the baby, but she also knew Michael was restless and needed answers. Perhaps when the baby arrived in a few weeks, he would settle down some, and just enjoy the baby. She imagined him spending time cuddling both the baby and her, taking time to change, clean, dress, and just watch the baby. Instead of seeking such deep answers, perhaps Michael would be the father she knew he would grow into, and love her and the baby just as a normal family.

The sun hung like a burning jewel, intent on setting the Israeli horizon on fire with its ominous presence. The desert, with the Galilean hills on the far edge, was lit up with fire and blue skies. A crow glared unforgiving into the distance. Its eyes had witnessed the very essence of life and death in this rough environment. Out here, in his world, life and death was not a matter of sheer chance. It was quite simply survival of the fittest, or the sickest. As in most life forms, survival came down to how far one is willing to go to be the survivor. On this day he was the survivor. Now, as he sat perched on top of one of the two thousand year old olive trees, left from when Jesus of Nazareth had walked this way with twelve followers and a crowd of on lookers, a crowd was gathering outside a small house. The crow however, had fought his battles for the day, at least so far, and had won. He was now staring into the distance, as if he could see some seventy-five miles away into Jerusalem, where life went on for the idiot human race, and events were beginning to unfold that would affect all humanity.

A baby was born. A virgin, named Mary gave birth to her first born son, and he was called Jesus. In a modest room, with only a mid-wife, two television cameras, a sound man, three doctors, and Brother Bob standing proudly to the side, a baby boy came into the world. Outside a cow moaned and some sheep bleated. A crow was heard to caw.

The baby looked around after it had sucked at his mother's breast. With blue eyes seeming to know everything from all eternity, he looked up at Brother Bob and smiled. He giggled and fell asleep in his mother's arms.

Brother Bob wept. He was the first man to look into the very eyes of God for over two thousand years. This was the edge of eternity and Jesus the Christ had returned to earth. He returned his gaze to the baby's face, a face that seemed to change and grow before his eyes. Somehow, the growth manipulation in the cloning process was indeed speeding up the rate of development.

The baby looked into his mother's eyes and as his mouth moved, Jesus said, "Momma".

Chronicles of the Shroud

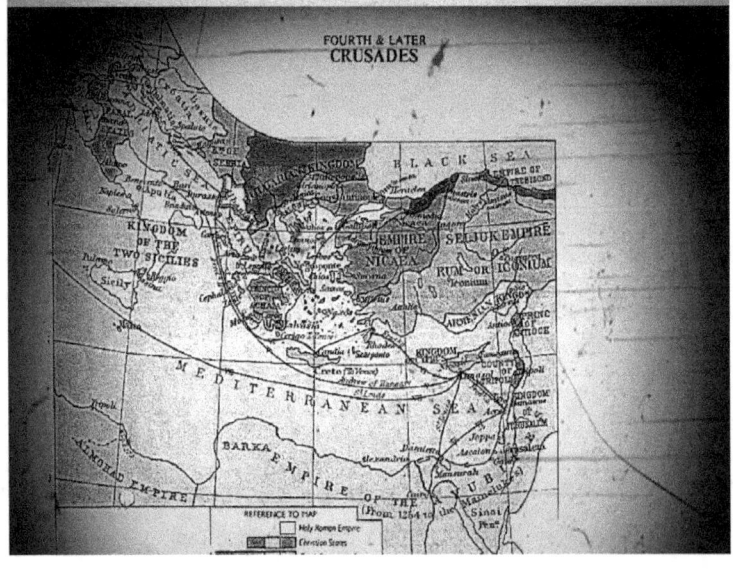

Appendix 1

Report from Father Jerome to Samuel, Pope Francis Paul.

Three months ago you asked me to seek the Truth about the possibility of the imminent return of our Lord Jesus. I have spent that time diligently seeking what might be happening among all the Christians around the world, searching databases, websites, and talking to friends and contacts in all nations. This is what I have discovered:

1. There have been many false claims through the centuries. It seems even today in our modern age more churches and leaders seem to make these claims that they have been told by God that now is the time for the return of the Lord. All of these claims have been proven false.

2. However, there is one Protestant preacher who is bolstered in confidence and placing his entire ministry and empire on the line. He declared several months ago from his pulpit in a mega church in Houston, Texas, in the USA, that God had told him that he (the preacher Brother Bob) would not die before he saw the return of the Lord Jesus. Since that time he has refocused his entire being and works on this project.

   He has developed a special team led by one, Brian Sharp (more on him later), to develop plans and contingencies for such an event. He also has a sincere and large following as well as a huge amount of money.

Since his initial sermon he has bought and now controls most of the major media outlets in America and thus throughout the world. His media empire focuses the world's attention on the need for a savior, showing that there is a need for the second coming.

There is a strong connection with Israel. The ministry owns several huge parcels of land in Israel (unheard of for a church to be allowed to purchase land in the Jewish state) and buildings of all sorts have been established there.

Then about six months ago a special object was brought to the church. Since that object arrived, a distinct veil of secrecy has fallen over the ministry. But miracles have begun. People with all types of ailments are being healed and made whole. These are not actors (as some preachers use), but these are documented cases of sickness, illness, life threatening diseases, psychological issues, and emotional problems. These are well documented by leading physicians. These healings are shown on their television program. It is as if the power of the Lord has returned, and He is healing as the stories in the New Testament tell us he healed when He walked the earth.

3. It seems a women connected to the church is pregnant and she is shrouded in much secrecy. She is in one of the compounds in Israel. I have heard from several (but with no definitive proof) that she might be carrying a baby cloned from the DNA of Jesus.

Implications of these things thus far:

1. If somehow this man has cloned Jesus, and since he owns a worldwide media and religious empire, he will have a very strong platform to spew his version of his truth and biblical views. This could lead to power struggles in churches and religions and thus cause wars.

2. He will have the power to undermine any other ministry, church organization, and every true work of the Lord including our church simply by using this vast power and platform

3. If he has indeed cloned Jesus many questions begged to be asked:

    Will the clone be the Son of God?

    Will he be able to perform miracles?

    Will he be holy and righteous, working for the Kingdom of God?

    Will he be sinless?

    Will he use his power for his own empire, prestige, and glory?

    Will he have power or be only human?

4. How can and will Brother Bob use this clone for his own ministry and kingdom?

Brian Sharp (Brother Bob's right hand man):

1. He seems to be a man chasing after his own version of his truth, and his version of the kingdom of God

2. He has sold clone material to Omega (a mercenary organization controlled by a man who desires to

crusade only for the kingdom of God). A massive army is being developed from these clones. Complete implications of this are unimaginable.

3. This man is someone who will do anything and has built a powerful system so that he is in control.

4. With such a man in control of the clone, of the ministry of Brother Bob, and his desire to see the world follow his version of God, this is a man to contend with. We should not ignore this man.

We were able to get into the computer system of this ministry. This is what we have learned:

> There seems to be a couple in Serbia that Brian Sharp is following and quite concerned about. She is carrying a baby.
>
> Why is Sharp concerned about this couple and baby?
>
> Who is this couple?
>
> We must work hard to keep an eye on this couple and discover more.

So, my brother, to return to your initial request of seeking what is happening regarding the return of our Lord:

1. There seems to be something happening with this church in Texas. We do not know precisely what is happening, but we must remain concerned about this.

2. If a clone, or many clones, of Jesus are on the earth today, we have major problems. Is this the

Son of God? Should we follow Him? Or is this the antichrist? Is this just a cloned man? Doctrinally we have major questions.

3. Is this couple in Serbia also pregnant with a clone? How did this happen and what are the implications of two clones of Jesus on the earth?

4. If an army of Jesus clones is produced, I cannot conceive of the power such an army will claim and wield over any government and country it desires to move on.

What must we in the Church do?

1. Pray: for wisdom, enlightenment, discernment, hope

2. We must not be fooled (we are told this too many times in the New Testament) by anything NOT of the Lord. But how to discern what is of God and what is not of God?

3. We must refocus the Church strongly on biblical teachings of the second coming of the Lord Jesus Christ.

My brother, you are the leader for such a time as this. I do not envy you the position you have. Know that I will always stand with you as my friend, my Pope. I do pray for wisdom for you.

Appendix 2

Diary from Mohammed Faisal

I sit here in my room and I am scared. A raven just cawed outside my window. I do not know if that is a good or bad sign. I think it is bad. I am scared, more scared than when I was little and I knew my father was going to whip my brother and me.

The past several months my team and I were sent to research about the possibility of Jesus Messiah returning to earth. Rumors had been heard and the leaders wanted to know what might be happening in the Christian Zionist West.

I am scared because of what I discovered. The formal report was given to the council and all was good, but this is the report I wanted to make but could not. I did not want to bring dishonor on our families and on the Prophet to tell the truth of what we found.

Jesus, the Son of God is returning soon! There, I have written the blasphemy that will end my life. This truth has already ended the four others on my team. Before my life ends, I must write the truth and the story I discovered.

We began by using parts of the internet that are not open to others in our country. We discovered Brother Bob and his ministry in Houston, Texas. After reading and finding all we could about him, we traveled to Texas to see for ourselves what was happening.

We had read that he believed with all his being that he would not die before Jesus returned to earth. In fact, he had placed all his resources, people, focus, money, and time and effort to this belief. He seemed to really believe this vision from God. We discovered something had happened several months ago that changed the character of the church. People were being healed, restored, miracles happening, thousands were changing their lives for this man and his belief.

Sub churches were popping up all over America and then the world with his messages coming via satellite to tell these people of the return of Jesus. Many other churches were being taken over by Brother Bob and his ministry. The media in America was focused on how the need for a savior was strong, and that Jesus was the answer needed all over the world.

Other religious groups were put down and even some followers of Buddha, Islam, and Satan worship were killed when their meeting places were destroyed. The police were not intervening to protect these non-Christian people. Books were being burned in public. Politicians seemed to be getting scared to say anything against the return of Jesus.

So we travelled to Texas and met with the leaders, and even met with Brother Bob. I must say he is a sincere and humble man. He seems to truly believe he is right and all others, like us, are wrong. He tried to convert us. We met with members and they were deep and committed followers of Brother Bob and his message.

I must say that having studied in America for 8 years in university; I had never found such committed believers in those years. Something has changed for these people and they believe with their hearts and actions. When I studied there were many who went to church but did not believe. Now those who go to church (and all churches we saw over the course of many weeks researching in America) were full and overflowing with people standing at doors and windows.

Something has been found by these people. Miracles, healings, changes in lives are happening. I saw many of them.

We stayed for 4 months. We talked to people at the church, in the media empire, and then we travelled to North Carolina to talk to people at Omega. We were not allowed to officially talk to anyone. But we met late one night at a bar in New Bern. Several men came and told us that the company is in the process of developing a massive army of clones from the DNA of Jesus. This army will destroy all that are not of God, and will not be stopped. They were only a few years away from moving the army to attack around the world.

This scared all of us. We had not really talked among ourselves until that night when we were in a hotel overlooking the river in New Bern. While we sat on the fourth floor balcony overlooking the marina, we talked and admitted our fears for Islam, our souls, and our families.

Two of the group admitted they were close to converting to Christianity. They had seen that everything they had been told while here at home in Iran was falsehood compared to the truth and sincerity of the Christians we had met. Mohammed Adzul and I talked into the night trying to change their minds. We parted after we prayed.

The next morning these two were gone. We could not find them; they did not answer their phones, and had simply disappeared. My partner and I began the trip home in sadness. We did not talk in any way as we were both wrapped up in our thoughts about all we had discovered, the possible movement of God, our two brothers committing heresy and converting to Christianity and dishonoring their families and religion. We flew to London.

We stayed in a hotel for a few days in London to begin to write our report. One morning I went to Mohammed's room and found him hanging from the ceiling. His note said that he had begun to believe in the Christ and that in order not to dishonor his family, he had to kill himself. I wept profusely.

So I have returned to my offices here in Tehran to write my report. I gave the official report this afternoon to the council. But now I complete this report of the real truth as I discovered it in Texas.

I hope to escape to Houston. For I too believe. I believe that this Christ is my Savior and Messiah.

Allen & Sword

<u>Works Cited</u>

Balkan Worlds: The First and Last Europe, by Traian Stoianovich. Armonk, NY: me Sharpe, 1994. 433 pp. ISBN: 1-56324-032-7

The Balkans since 1453. L.S. Stavrainos. Professor of History, Northwastern University. Holt, Rinehart and Winston October, 1963.

These two texts are the definitive works on Balkan history and the texts I studied in graduate school.

http://en.wikipedia.org/wiki/Shroud_of_Turin

Chronicles of the Fourth Crusade, Jean de Joinville, Penquin classics, 2009, 384 pp. ISBN – 10 0140449981.

www.compulsory.com/maps/Europe/Serbia

http://europeancrusaders.worspaces.com

<u>Acknowledgements</u>

This book is over five years in the creating, writing and resting. I was moving a sailboat from Savannah, GA to NC. Jerry gave me the simple idea: "what would happen if someone got the DNA of Jesus and cloned him?" I thought and pondered this for 5 days as I moved my boat north. When I got to homeport, I was able to write the story you hold in your hands.

It was a labor of love, frustration, allowing it to rest and grow for a few years, and then attacking the story afresh.

Mary Klaus (and her daughter Gretchen Latimer), my dear friend from teaching days has kindly read, edited and given critical suggestions. They have done a tremendous job, but any errors are mine.

My parents, Al and JoAnne have always given simple and profound encouragement to me. Friends far and near, through time and years have been my strength. Special friends have read and added comments. Friends who have influenced and helped me in life are: Eric, Rhonda, Jeremiah, YY, my brother Calvin and his entire family, Robert and Pavel. Thank you each very much.

The real Sladjana is always the lady and friend I can lean on.

Early mornings, late nights on my boat (where I live) when I write and create; have allowed this to happen.

Now we begin to continue the story into book two of the series. Stay tuned to the webpage for all that happens.

-Stefan

I am not really certain where I should begin with the acknowledgements; however I feel certain that I should begin with expressing my extreme gratitude to Stefan for believing in the story that began floating around in my mind a few years ago. You are a true friend and mentor, and I am very happy that you and I are taking this journey together.

I am also thankful to our editor Mary Klaus; and our publisher Full Moon Publishing LLC, for believing in this project as well. The truth is that there are so many people to thank that I won't remember all of you at the time of writing this. Above all I thank God for allowing us to offer our take on the end of the world. I thank my sister Carol for holding my hand through the roughest spots in my life, and I thank my mother for believing in the ridiculous undertakings I put upon myself. As always I love you Jonathan, and I am grateful for everyone who has believed in this project in the many forms it has taken throughout its journey into print. Hope, thank you for tolerating all the hours I put into these things.

See you next time

JS

AUTHOR BIOS

Stefan T. Allen is the pen name of a man who has spent almost 20 years in education (secondary and university). He has worked on four continents and visited 54 countries. Currently he lives on a boat in eastern NC. He writes short stories and poetry. He reads profusely and enjoys watching the sun set with a glass of wine and sitting on the top of his boat.

Jerry Sword is a songwriter, filmmaker, and author from Virginia. His works have been featured in motion pictures as well as independent features. He currently resides and continues writing in a small Virginia town.

Allen & Sword

www.ingramcontent.com/pod-product-compliance
Lightning Source LLC
Chambersburg PA
CBHW070035260626
47159CB00005B/2048